Murphy's Miracle

One Dog's Wild Journey

Murphy's Miracle

One Dog's Wild Journey

JULIE SAMRICK

Artwork by Susan Krupp
Published by Motina Books

Murphy's Miracle
One Dog's Wild Journey

Copyright ©2018 by Julie Samrick
All rights reserved.

No part of this publication may be reproduced, distributed or
transmitted in any form or by any means, or stored in a database
or retrieval system, without the prior written permission of the
publisher.

Published by Motina Books, Allen, Texas.
http://www.MotinaBooks.com

Illustrations by Susan Krupp
http://www.yuneekpix.com

Edited by Ashley Schmidt
http://www.StacksByAshley.com

Library of Congress Cataloging-in-Publication Data
Samrick, Julie.
  Murphy's Miracle : One Dog's Wild Journey / Julie Samrick
2018936999

ISBN-13: 978-1-945060-10-6
ISBN-10: 1-945060-10-7

This story was inspired by true events. Some names and
identifying details have been changed to protect the privacy of
the individuals.

For the Brauns, because they never gave up hope.

CONTENTS

Between every two pine trees there is a door leading to a new way of life.

~ John Muir

Prologue

October, 2012

Murphy was trembling. Her whole body shook, from her nose to the tip of her tail. The five-year-old golden retriever ran from the explosive noises, farther and farther into the forest. Her quick movements soon separated her from her human family, with whom she had been camping just moments before.

Her breathing came fast as she deftly maneuvered around obstacles blocking her way, tall trees and a mish-mash of rocks. She darted past them like she knew the place well.

Lungs heaving, Murphy panted. Every cell in her body pounded as she remained on high alert. Even if she wanted to, Murphy's body couldn't slow down, not until the sharpness in her ears dulled. Oh, how she wished for the deafening sounds to stop! Finally, only then, would she be able to stop racing, and her heartbeat would slow from a racing tick, tick, tick to a more gradual tick…tock…tick…tock.

Everything slowed as Murphy walked deeper into the Eldorado National Forest in Northern California, a dense forest that lies at the base of the Sierra Nevada mountain range. Each step that she took into the shrouded woods was another barrier that separated her from her family and the comforts that she loved in the safety of her home. Each step created a deeper divide between herself and just about all other living beings. That is, except for the most threatening animals, the ones that live in the forest. Murphy would soon find herself all alone with the things that howl at the moon and the ones that must eat ravenously to fall asleep.

When she eventually stopped walking the sugar pine trees were so dense they hardly allowed any sunlight in. In the stillness, she looked side to side, taking in her new surroundings for the first time.

Murphy whined, aware that she was all alone. Her tail drooped and she was overcome with defeat. She felt uneasy without her family and the warmth of their home, the place she would rather be than anywhere else in the world.

There was a rustling sound and then a teasing, "Coo-coo," that came from above. Murphy's heart leaped at the sound of another living thing. She'd forgotten her apprehension by then, her nose sniffing the air to identify what made this pleasant, curious noise. The scents of the forest were unfamiliar, but Murphy was eager to learn more about this mysterious new place as the smell of bark and pine enveloped her.

The cooing sound stopped just as quickly as it had started. Murphy's ears, which moments before had been on alert, relaxed, drooping back down at once. She looked up at the huge canopy of trees that blocked the sun's bright rays and lowered her head, breathing in the ground as she took in more clues, savoring the soil, damp and musky.

Murphy's nose led her away from the cluster of pine trees until she was back under the open sky and nearly to a river's edge. The scents of other animals were strong at the riverbank; their waste, their skin, their fur, an individual story attached to each one. Visions flooded Murphy's mind with the flurry of smells, lingering from the creatures that had been in that spot, possibly moments before.

There was something light, something dark, something menacing, and something defenseless; a still shot of each whizzed through her mind like the confusing, dizzying sights taken in while on a rollercoaster ride.

Murphy's eye caught a flash 15 feet away across the narrow channel of water on the riverbank. It was a fish that floundered on land, drowning in air, just one, short, wrong jump out of the water. In years past, before California's historic drought, rivers and lakes across the state held more water. But now dirt and rocks lay exposed where water would have covered it otherwise.

Murphy was unaware that the fish was in danger.

A playmate! was her first thought.

The twitching fish was a sight more enticing than the water, which beckoned Murphy to take a cool drink from it.

But just then, something else moved, leading Murphy's eye to it, forgetting the fish on land just as quickly. It was a fish as well, but this one had much more energy than the former as it jumped out from under the sparkling surface with vigor. Not knowing it was being watched, the fish may as well have been signaling a "peek-a-boo, come get me" motion to Murphy.

Fatigue forgotten, as well as the first fish, which didn't seem to have the same enthusiasm to play, Murphy wagged her tail in greeting, running side to side mere inches from the water, not taking her eyes off her gliding, hopefully new, companion.

Murphy dodged when the fish leaped into the air.

I'm here! Murphy relayed as she paced and wagged her tail. *Look at me!* She hopped and even whimpered a bit, trying to get the frisky little fish to look at her.

Eyes wide, Murphy watched the fish slip under the water and so she stopped mid-step, impatiently waiting for it to jump out again. As her heart beat with anticipation, Murphy's eyes didn't move, laser-focused on the water's surface.

While all of this joy and revelry was taking place, the fish on land had surrendered its last breaths and was finally still. Yet Murphy hadn't noticed. Her mind had been glued to the very lively little friend in front of her instead.

The fish wasn't close enough but Murphy wasn't concerned; she waded into the river to get closer. She nosed the water, splashing her eyes and jowls, startling herself as much as she had the silver beauty, making it instinctively flit away.

The fish didn't evade her for long. It turned and was back in her presence, moving to the same rhythm under the water as Murphy was above it. They moved back and forth, mirror images of one another. The fish seemed as eager to play as Murphy was and that got her heartbeat racing once more.

With this wonderful distraction, Murphy forgot the gnawing hunger that wouldn't let go, tugging at her insides and relentlessly pleading with her to satisfy it. Murphy kept on playing in spite of it.

Murphy hadn't eaten since Nathan had fed her last, but flashes of his voice and face made her believe, in fleeting moments, that he was near. She would wag her tail in greeting and look side to side, only to see tall trees and hear the cool mountain breeze that tickled her face. Where was Nathan now? She couldn't find him, her master, whose commands she had always followed and whose voice had always made it known whether it was time to take direction or play. For Murphy, no Nathan meant no food and no security. In those moments of realization Murphy lowered her head and lay down, without the enthusiasm to investigate.

Until she found the fish to play with, Murphy had been nervous, restless even. Once she stopped running from the deafening blasts, and realized she was without her family, she whimpered, her amber eyes forlorn.

This wasn't the first time she had felt unnerved like this. No, Murphy didn't like to be alone in the least. She hated it when her family would gather their things and walk out of their home's front door. It was then, in an instant, that the family home went from a place of comfort to loneliness, from lightness to dark.

Murphy could always tell when her family was getting ready to leave. Keys would jangle and there would be a flurry of activity. They would congregate at the closet to retrieve their coats and the children's voices would rise near the bathroom. "Let me go first," they would say. When someone else went into the bathroom, the door would slam and the others would groan and knock on it.

"Come on, let's go," Erin or Nathan would say and walk to the door. Murphy sensed in their voices and actions that something was going on. Their voices always showed leadership and Murphy liked to hear them talk best. If all went well, Erin or Nathan would say the word, "walk," which gave her a thrill like nothing else. When someone went to grab her leash she couldn't hold back her excitement. Often when her family would gather by the door, collecting coats and shoes, Murphy would pace with them, waiting to hear that wonderful "W" word, only to hear them say, "Bye, girl," instead.

But she never gave up hope that she would hear the word that equaled freedom and adventure. Until she heard anything else, Murphy would wait by the door and listen for someone to say, "Walk," or "Come on girl!"

Whenever the door shut and Murphy was left alone, she would feel the urge to chew on something. Usually the easiest things to find were the soft objects that have laces on them, those things that her family had so many of and which were always on the ground, easy to get. Yes, those would do.

But in the forest Murphy looked, but couldn't find anything like the soft objects to chew.

She'd certainly felt the same urge as back at home, anxious in her loneliness. In fact, just before she saw the happy fish Murphy had been nibbling on some bark.

Now, her loneliness forgotten, Murphy's eyes lit up as she watched the fish's movement and she smiled in the way dogs do. Without touching, Murphy and the fish continued to move to their own rhythm like they were performing a perfectly practiced dance.

They frolicked together on their own stage, Murphy on land while the fish remained in the water, when suddenly the carefree moment was interrupted.

A force rudely pushed Murphy from behind, thrusting her out of the way and knocking her into the water.

Murphy's eyes remained glued to the spot where her friend had been, but the ripples on the water's surface made it difficult to see her playmate any longer.

Suddenly, an enormous black bear bounded past Murphy like he needed saving from fire. In reality the bear wasn't in danger or even uncomfortable. He just wanted something very specific, something much more interesting to him than Murphy.

As the bear edged deeper in, the water reached his barrel-sized stomach. Within seconds, he deftly pulled his cinnamon colored paw out of the water, with a thrashing fish in his clutches; the same delightful fish that had been so happy and calm as it danced with Murphy only moments before.

Murphy watched the fish flop in the bear's grasp, but then it was gone, swallowed by the bear in an instant.

Murphy instinctively barked at the bear. *That was my friend*, she hoped to communicate.

The bear looked back at her and roared. The heat of his breath was a clear warning. *Back off, little puppy!* the bear bellowed.

Murphy whimpered and her tail drooped, barking a little softer. *Why did you take it away?*

He glared at Murphy and it became clear who was in charge. *You don't know who you're messing with*, the bear's eyes blazed.

Just as Murphy averted her gaze, the bear turned to look at the water's rolling surface. His hunting eye keen, he waited two blinks, then dashed his face and paws into the water to grab one more sashimi appetizer. Murphy stayed glued to her spot.

Still not satisfied, the bear sprang across the narrow channel to the other shore. His sight was set on the beached fish, lifelessly staring out of its one exposed eye.

Unfazed, the bear tossed that fish down in one gulp too, then turned toward Murphy as if to dare, *What are you gonna do about it?*

Murphy's tail sank between her legs and she released a nervous whine in return. She now understood that the bear was the leader in this exchange and knew it would be wiser to act harmless, just as she acted with virtually all other animals. In fact, Murphy actually preferred to be on a leash; it made her feel safe. Whenever she took a walk with her family and saw another dog, Murphy would always look away if the animal exuded the slightest strength. Only when they were camping did she feel the confidence to explore.

Could you at least play with me? Murphy began to communicate to the bear with a yelp, but felt fear just as soon as she made the half-hearted request.

The bear looked at her, eyes narrowed, while Murphy's heart and legs froze with dread. She didn't know what to do, but the bear, the brutish leader in this exchange, decided for them both. He slowly turned and lumbered back up the riverbank the way he had come. Stomach satisfied for at least the time being, the bear was no doubt making last preparations before his long winter's nap.

Meanwhile, Murphy was left standing alone without a fish, or anyone, to play with and her growing hunger made her feel even worse. She nibbled at some moss and then turned her attention to chewing on a bit of bark that had peeled off a tree. Little toothpicks of wood jabbed her gums, but the solidness of the bark settled her stomach and made her forget her loneliness for the time being.

Once her stomach wasn't beating like a drum and her gums ached from the shards of wood, Murphy resumed walking and continued to follow the water's edge. Its power faded from a bubbling river to a muddy creek the farther she got from her family, other animals, and seemingly the rest of the world.

By dusk Murphy was enclosed within a dense patch of pine trees, tall and majestic, silent witnesses to the secrets the woods have kept for centuries. As she traveled deeper into the forest, the trees began to eclipse the sun until daytime was as dark and lonely as the night.

For generations, the occasional hunter would make it this far into the woods and stand against a tree, waiting for forest animals to make themselves known for capture. There are hundreds, even thousands, of species of birds in this region of the United States. Species range from quail, doves, and pigeons to Canada geese, golden eagles, mountain chickadee, red-shafted flicker, and fox sparrows.

Despite a snack of bark here or a bite of foliage there, Murphy's stomach kept rumbling like a cruel bully that just wouldn't stop pestering her.

She still didn't know where her family was, but even when she was home without them there were still certain comforts that she would enjoy. In the forest there was no easy water to drink, no quick laps from the silver bowl she had grown accustomed to. There were no quick tosses of popcorn for her to catch in her mouth and certainly no warm shelter, a shelter made even cozier once her family reunited with her each afternoon and evening to give her affection and plenty to eat.

Dried brush continued to collect on Murphy's paws as she walked slowly, legs stiffening, her limbs begging to collapse with each step.

Her muscles cramped until she couldn't take another step. She lay down at the foot of a tree, aware that her left front paw ached. She licked it and tasted the coppery flavor of blood. She washed herself before resting a while.

Since her encounter with the bear, Murphy didn't see another animal until late the next evening. She sensed something was near, her tail perking up as she stood. A lone squirrel scurried up the trunk of a tall tree. Murphy followed her instinct to run toward it. The gray squirrel was swift, moving up and up, shielding itself behind branches while Murphy's eyes followed. Murphy's mouth was dry, but her hunger and loneliness were unbearable.

The little squirrel, and Murphy's impulse to run after it, was the shot of adrenaline she needed to keep going. She forgot her pain and the squirrel took Murphy's mind back to her own yard, where she had a habit of intently watching the same critters that teetered skillfully along the fence line. Whenever one stopped to vault onto a tree branch, Murphy would stand at attention and spring after it, hoping to play.

This forest squirrel stopped and turned, holding something in its clutches. Murphy stood at attention, keeping her eyes on it until it vanished somewhere in the tree, way up high.

Her bronze-colored head turned up, and Murphy heard the now familiar coo-coo, the same whistling sound that perked her ears before. The squirrel was forgotten.

Her senses alert, Murphy tilted her head to see a somewhat large bird on the ground a short distance away. It had a short, fat bill and a long, rounded tail. It was a Bachman's Sparrow, which can be hard to see because they cleverly camouflage with their surroundings.

The whirring from above sounded again, only louder; it was a mama bird in distress. Having fallen from the nest, the baby sparrow settled just feet away. Its light gray face and upper body blended into the earth. Only its yellow legs stood out in contrast, making it possible for Murphy to see it. Murphy edged toward the helpless chick. Its live smell wasn't one she'd normally find irresistible, but Murphy's hunger was relentless, punching her viciously by then. When Murphy looked at the creature, so still and defenseless, she didn't see a playmate. No, not at all. Actually, when she looked at the little, trembling bird, Murphy saw dinner.

She bent her head down to clutch the little bird's belly in her mouth. Then Murphy trotted to a clearing to lay beneath a tree with the baby bird still held tightly between her jaws, its feathers filling her mouth. So weak, the baby bird barely moved by then. From a distance, its mother continued to cry.

Murphy had been raised with the finest things of domestic dog life. She'd only known table scraps, tummy rubs, walks on a leash and, her favorite thing—lots of kisses planted just between her eyes.

Yet the days of easy, highchair scraps were over. Murphy wasn't a housedog any longer. She would have to survive in the wild, and this meant that whether she ate or not would be up to her.

Her teeth sank into the bird. And with that bite, Murphy knew the aching, tiresome feeling of hunger was something she would need to satisfy. Whenever she encountered another living thing in this new, unfamiliar land, it would have to be sized up not only for its potential to be a playmate, but even more importantly, she would need to discern if it would satisfy her unrelenting, ravenous hunger.

Chapter 1

At first things were smooth leading up to the camping trip Murphy took with her father, Nathan Braun, and the oldest child, 10-year-old Matthew. That Friday after lunch, father and son and their best friends left their Northern California homes near Sacramento to drive east on Highway 80, caravanning single-file in off-road Jeeps without a care in the world. It was supposed to be one of the trips the men had enjoyed for years. They had been taking camping trips together since long before any of them had become fathers and now their children joined them too.

Murphy was the latest in a long line of dogs to go on the trip and she loved camping just as much as Matthew did, maybe even more. The smells and the freedom to roam made her eyes gleam and her tail wag enthusiastically. In the outdoors Murphy would sniff constantly, breathing in new stories with her nose like a detective studying clues. Still, just like the boys and the men, Murphy's favorite smells of all were fresh bacon frying and the clear mountain air. She'd turn her nose upward and savor the deliciousness with anticipation.

Murphy was the only dog on that particular camping adventure. Her dog sister, the family's other golden retriever, stayed home with Erin and the younger Braun children, who included eight-year-old Morgan and baby Finegan.

At 10 years old, Matthew was deemed old enough for camping in Desolation Wilderness. He liked video games, but he'd trade them for outdoor adventures with his dad and friends any day. He had never joined Boy Scouts, but because of all the camping trips with his dad, Matthew knew as much about outdoor survival as any boy his age. The badges Matthew earned on these outdoor trips were badges of pride and of making new memories with his father.

After an hour of driving the group exited Highway 80 in Foresthill, a small, one-stoplight town at the foot of the Sierra Nevada Mountains. The men and two boys jumped out to stretch at Worton's Market, their usual stop at the last place to get snacks, gasoline, and to use a clean restroom before the first part of their adventure would begin, driving Jeeps down the bumpy Rubicon Trail to hidden campgrounds.

Nathan couldn't have been more comfortable with these men if they had actually been blood brothers. He couldn't know them any better either. They knew each other's characters, their strengths as well as their weaknesses, and accepted them whole-heartedly. Friends for 20 years, they had been through life's greatest challenges and joys with one other. They'd been single together, then married, and even saw one of the guys in their group of friends through a divorce. Not quite 40 years old, they'd had their share of health issues too. Out of the five of them, one of the men had Type-1 diabetes; there were back and knee problems among them and even a stroke. Yet Nathan, so healthy at first impression, perhaps had the most worrisome health history of any of the men. He had suffered a heart attack less than a year before, just a few weeks before their baby, Finegan, was born. And that had been his second heart attack; the first one had been when he was only 33 years old. Through it all, Nathan's friends remained a devoted band of brothers there to see him and Erin through it.

What made these camping trips priceless was that because of their collective struggles, the men enjoyed their downtime together in the outdoors even more. The laughs and the new memories were like medicine for some of the biggest pains in their lives.

Nathan knew as much about loss as any of the men. The youngest of four children, things hadn't come easy to him as a child. As his father and mother struggled to make ends meet, Nathan learned he had to work, and work hard, for anything he wanted in life. While some teenagers are given keys to a brand-new car at 16 years old, Nathan earned the money to buy a used pickup truck. While the most work many kids had to do was fill their gas tanks with their parents' credit cards, Nathan always paid for his own gas; he learned how to fix his car, too.

When he was 21 he and Erin met selling cell phones back when cell phones were luxury items. They had a friendship first and foremost, and never lost sight of that.

It was a good thing he had Erin by his side. What was supposed to be the most wonderful time in their lives—an engagement, planning for a wedding, and thinking about a long future together—was marred by sadness. Just two weeks before their wedding, Nathan's father died at only 58 years old. He had been up on a ladder, just trimming a tree in the backyard as he had done so many times before, when he fell to the ground, having suffered a massive heart attack.

Nathan and Erin stood by his mother's side, helping her through those early days as she navigated being a widow. Nathan, by then a new husband, and barely a grown man himself, took his father's death as a reminder to take care of his own health. He was vigilant about exercising and remembered to eat well most of the time. He took pride in how he minded his health and so it came as a shock, when in another cruel twist of fate, Nathan suffered a heart attack when he was only 33 years old and then again when he was 36. The second time Erin was nearly nine months pregnant with Finegan, their third child and a pleasant surprise after thinking their baby years were behind them. Morgan and Matthew were seven and eight years old by then.

"It's in the genes," the doctors told Nathan after the second heart attack, but those words did nothing to change the way he felt. Nathan was angry and often thought, *This isn't fair.* But no amount of frustration would change his circumstances; he could only control how he reacted to them. He understood that the only thing he had control over was to not take his family, or his health, for granted, because each and every day is a blessing.

Together Erin and Nathan had learned sooner than most people that life has its hurdles, so their way of life was to cherish it by not worrying about petty things, but to spend time with the people they loved most—their children, their extended family, their friends, and to make new memories whenever they could.

Their dogs were an extension of this belief. Erin and Nathan always had two dogs at a time, and not just any dogs. They always had their favorite breed— golden retriever. Murphy was the fifth golden retriever they had had in their marriage, but little did they know she might be their last.

Chapter 2

"It won't start," Nathan muttered as his engine turned over but wouldn't catch during their stop at Worton's Market. *The last place to get gas and snacks might be the end of the trip, period,* he thought, disappointed.

He looked out the front window and saw Matthew and Ryan's son, Joey, leading Murphy around the parking lot by a leash, stretching their legs as they killed time. Matthew looked so much like Nathan did at the same age. He had the same dark brown, wavy hair and though Nathan's hair had thinned over the years, father and son still shared the same shy smile. Murphy seemed to be the one leading the way. She walked quickly, stopping every few feet to smell, as the boys were pulled right along with her, stopping whenever she did.

So many different people and animals here before,

Murphy thought, deep into the detective work she loved whenever she was in a new place. Dictated to her entirely by smell alone, her nose allowed her to lace together the different stories while her heart thumped in anticipation, wondering what clues she'd discover next.

She stopped to sniff a tree. Another animal had just been here...*Maybe it's still here*, she thought, raising her head to check her surroundings.

Murphy walked a few steps before she stopped again. She sensed a different animal this time, something unfamiliar and wild. Her tail wagged as she tried to determine the story, the possibilities, that came with the foreign scent.

She followed it to a tin garbage can overflowing with chip bags, burrito wrappers, and half-full cups of discarded drinks. Murphy breathed in the ground until something else grabbed her attention, making her forget the mysterious aroma in an instant She was overpowered by something sweet that she could smell and taste. She savored whatever it was—a child's spilled ice cream or a syrupy drink. She licked in and around the area for any trace of the sugary droplets, paying no mind to the dirt she lapped up with it.

Once there was no more delicious syrup to be had, Murphy pulled on the leash to walk to a clearing where she squatted to do her business. Matthew and Joey laughed at the funny dog's lack of modesty.

Back at the Jeep, nothing could amuse Nathan. He felt discouraged about his Jeep not starting and wrestled in his mind about what to do next. Before he got out to take a look his mind raced, coming up with dozens of possibilities about what the problem could be and what he could do to fix it.

I'll call a tow truck, he thought. It was an ominous sign that his Jeep had broken down before it did the much harder work that was ahead. *We'll head home…*

Then he thought of Matthew, a disappointed look on his face, and just as quickly Nathan thought, *Nah…everyone will be let down. There's got to be something else I can do.*

Next to him a truck pulled up and a young man was slowly moving to get out of it. A small ramp thudded as the man dropped it and then deftly picked up his legs to move his body into a wheelchair.

Nathan tried not to stare, but was intrigued by the man trying to do something that most people don't even have to think about, let alone struggle with—to get out of a car.

What do I have to complain about, really? Nathan thought, his patience coming back for the task before him.

His mind returned to thinking about what could be wrong with the Jeep. He had a full tank of gas and he was pretty sure that the starter was working fine. He got out, propped up the hood, and began looking for anything that seemed to be out of place.

"When are we going Dad?" Matthew asked. "Do you think you can fix it?"

Nathan didn't answer and continued to try to

troubleshoot for the next 20 minutes. Finally, Nathan scratched his head. He was getting ready to call a tow truck when there was a tap on the Jeep's frame, inches from his face. Nathan turned to see a stranger, a man who looked like a vagrant, looking at him. The fraying patch on the man's shirt was inscribed with his name—Leo.

Leo's face was brushed with dirt and his clothes were even filthier. When he opened his mouth to speak, Nathan noticed the man was missing several teeth.

He probably wants money, Nathan thought, his patience waning.

But the man's eyes were bright and welcoming, sparkling blue swimming pools against the dark oil on his skin and clothes. "What's the problem?" he asked.

"Car won't start," Nathan mumbled, frustrated.

The man looked Nathan in the eye. "Want me to take a look?" he asked. Leo sounded confident that he could at least diagnose the problem, if not fix it.

Based on the man's appearance, Nathan was doubtful.

Murphy noticed the stranger with Nathan and pulled the boys in that direction. She wanted to inspect this new person and Matthew was left with no other choice but to follow as Murphy tugged the leash toward the stranger, pulling Matthew along.

Who is that with Dad? Murphy thought as she struggled to make her way toward Nathan.

The other men were inside the store, stocking up

on meat, cheese, and a long loaf of sourdough bread to make their customary huge sandwich to share.

Nathan pulled pliers and a screwdriver out of a toolbox and the two men studied the engine. Leo twisted to reach something on the side, then fiddled with something else before standing up straight, wiping his hands on his gray shirt.

Just as Nathan was about to tell the bad news to Matthew and Joey, that their trip was over just as it was starting, the man spoke.

"I'm pretty sure it's the coil," he told Nathan matter-of-factly.

Nathan was hopeful, but leaned forward to take a look.

"Where can I get a coil at this time of night?" Nathan asked.

"The nearest auto shop still open is 45 minutes away," Leo replied as he started to walk toward the store, stopping to wipe his forehead, smudging more grime on his weather-beaten skin. "I'm just on my way home from work, gettin' a bite...Holler if you need anything."

"Hey, let me buy your dinner," Nathan replied, still thinking this man could probably use any help he could get by the looks of him. "You didn't have to stop and help me."

"Nah," Leo waved him off.

Nathan double-checked the ignition coil and looked at his watch. It was past 5:00 p.m. He thought about what Leo had said, and knew there wouldn't be any auto shops open in Foresthill.

While explaining the situation to the group Nathan was interrupted mid-sentence when Mark, who everyone calls Bubba, said he'd drive the 45 miles to the closest large town, Auburn.

Bubba may have been the first one to volunteer, but any one of the guys would have done the same; that's the kind of friends they were. While a few things may have changed with the friends in the two decades they had known each other, one thing that never changed was that no matter how old they were, the fun they had together never stopped. It had simply evolved into a different kind of fun. After they all purchased dirt bikes, they collectively moved on to a motorcycle phase that lasted until they became fathers. That new chapter brought with it boats and off-roading vehicles, specifically Jeeps. Jeeping wasn't just a way for them to get to and from campsites; the off-road journeys they took to get there were adventures in their own right.

The main thing that was constant with the group of friends, even more than having fun, was that they were loyal—they would always have each other's backs.

Chapter 3

As the group hung out back at Worton's waiting for Bubba they ate hunks of the sandwich, passing the two-foot long creation around. Someone tore off a piece and then passed it to the others. This way of eating wouldn't have happened if their wives had been with them. The different aromas emanating from the sandwich were so strong that Murphy gazed into Matthew's eyes in a trance; she was panting, saliva forming around her open mouth, hoping and pleading for one small morsel. Matthew dropped a piece of ham, looking to see if his dad saw him do it. But Nathan had his back turned, too distracted to care about what Murphy was or wasn't eating.

Matthew heard his dad's voice talking with Ryan and Bubba, who had just returned with the part for the Jeep.

The three of them fiddled under the Jeep's hood like doctors performing surgery.

Nathan walked to the driver side and climbed in.

"Start 'er up!" Bubba called. He pushed the bill of his ragged baseball cap up to wipe his forehead with the back of his hand.

Hopeful, Nathan turned the key in the ignition. Instead of sputtering before it could catch as it had countless times that afternoon, this time the engine turned and then started. It was the best sound in the world to Nathan.

"Yes!" he shouted. "Thank you! Now let's get on that trailhead."

Matthew and Joey walked over and stretched their legs out to climb up before pitching themselves in over one side. They called to Murphy, who had settled next to Nathan's Jeep. She was at rest but ready to spring up at any moment like a good protector.

"Come on girl!" Matthew called from inside the car. Murphy quickly jumped up and leaped in, ready to continue the journey. She panted, eyes lit up, as she looked out.

I'm ready, she thought. *Let's go!*

Nathan's friends had remained as calm with the good news as they had when the engine wouldn't start. Steady personalities are good to have around, especially in a crisis.

Nathan's thoughts went to Leo, whom he figured was probably home by then. He was another guy who was willing to help someone in need without thinking twice. In that moment, Nathan couldn't help but think about his initial judgment of Leo as a homeless person, and thought of what his mom had always said about not judging a book by its cover.

Chapter 4

Bellies and gas tanks full, the camping group pulled off Interstate 80 in the dark to take a winding, unpaved road. Like a secret passage, each mile they drove into the wilderness brought them further away from their busy lives and closer to the calm they felt when they were with nature.

The group stopped at the base of the trailhead to slightly deflate their Jeep tires in order to make them more malleable to the human-size boulders which crowd the most famous off-roading trail in America. The "just right" amount of air in a Jeep's tires to traverse sharp rocks on the Rubicon Trail is when the tires are not flat, but also not so tight that rugged points could pop them on contact.

Driving off-road on the Rubicon Trail is something people from all over the world travel to do, but these experienced campers were there after the summer crowds had left. October is a quiet month on the Rubicon. It's the tail-end of the off-roading season because of the unpredictable weather. At 5,000 to 6,000 feet, an adventurer on the Rubicon could easily get caught in a rain or snow storm, making the already treacherous trip more dangerous. The Rubicon isn't as crowded as one might think at any time of the year, though, because a whole group of travelers is eliminated from the start. A regular truck doesn't have the strength to make it. Only those with Jeeps or other off-roading vehicles dare to make the journey.

Traveling the Rubicon is not an activity for the impatient traveler. The men knew to navigate it one by one, at a crawl, over and around each bulbous boulder. Just as a swimmer should never run on a wet pool deck, a Jeep must go slow down the trail so that it doesn't slip on the smooth granite rocks or worse, flip over. Another danger is shale—a razor-sharp rock that dots the Rubicon, and is an unrelenting enemy to the sturdiest vehicle's tires.

It would take hours to drive the short five miles to their campsite, but the boys and men loved every minute of it. They drove so slowly that a person could easily run past them and back, lapping their Jeeps several times.

Teamwork is a vital ingredient to make a successful journey out on the Rubicon. A driver should never attempt to make it alone. A passenger is as important as the driver because he or she serves as a guide. They act as the clear vision that drivers don't have otherwise.

Matthew was an experienced passenger. He would get out and run a little bit ahead to offer verbal and non-verbal commands for his father. Once he got far enough ahead so his whole body was in sight, Matthew would turn back around to signal with his voice and his arms stretched out straight like a ground controller on an airport runway.

Matthew understood his importance to the mission as he gave short commands. He walked backwards, facing the Jeep, which was inching towards him. Matthew's eyes remained focused on the vehicle's oversized wheels while Nathan's eyes remained on his son.

"Driver," Matthew would call, meaning his Dad should turn left, in the direction where the driver sits.

Then, "Passenger!" meaning, "Turn to the right!"

Within 10 minutes of beginning their slow descent down the trail, a small, tan pickup truck cruised past them. It was driving up on the shoulder to pass, speeding compared to how slowly Nathan and his friends had been rolling. The men and boys hung their mouths open in surprise.

As the truck passed, the driver and passenger smiled broadly and nodded hello. They were men with short black hair who were about the same age as Nathan and his friends.

The men in the pickup truck seemed at ease and

were either not aware of, or didn't care, that they were one sharp rock from being stranded, or worse.

Murphy barked at the sudden appearance of others who were not part of their group.

Hello there! her bark relayed.

Nathan flinched, taken aback by the truck's speed, but figured the men were in a rush to get somewhere.

Nathan and his friends patiently plodded on and didn't pass another vehicle for the next half hour. It was another sign that the off-roading season was coming to an end until the following year.

Just ahead they saw the same, tan truck pulled off to the left of the trail, and as they approached they saw that no one was inside. As Nathan and the others meandered past the empty truck, Matthew looked to the right side of the trail and saw a shotgun propped against a tree, with a bag of something next to it. He peered more closely and saw several gray tails sticking out of the bag, unmoving.

"They're hunting," Nathan said without taking his eyes off the unconventional road, a bead of sweat on his forehead as his whole body shifted sideways over one steep dip down. "Looks like they've done well."

Chapter 5

Just after dusk, the darkness continued to usher the group deeper into the forest. Bright headlights were crucial guides as they winded down, down, slow and careful. The children looked out the open rooftop, lulled by the dips and bumps just as a rocking cradle soothes a baby to sleep. Hardly a star could be seen because clouds blanketed the sky. A lightning bolt electrified the horizon for a second.

"Did you see that?" Matthew asked, his eyes wide, feeling a few drops of rain on his forehead. He pulled up the hood of his sweatshirt but was otherwise comfortable.

After passing the hunters they hadn't encountered anyone else. When someone had to go to the bathroom, there was no need to pull over. They just stopped where they were, or, if it was a passenger, he just walked to the side of the trail to go.

The Jeeps stopped mid-rock. There was no perfect place to park so they stopped wherever they were. The boys tumbled over the sides of the Jeep and Nathan coaxed Murphy out the back. "Go on girl," he said as Murphy jumped. She went straight to the woods where the scents of pine and other animals were strong. Her curiosity to inspect made her stall. Eyes bright and tongue wagging, Murphy searched her surroundings before settling on one lucky spot.

The shadow of the forest at sunset made it fully dark, yet with a dog's clear nighttime vision, Murphy bounded back to the group easily while the kids stayed close to the trail, turning backs on one another for privacy.

Murphy's tail wagged, eyes still smiling, as she looked up at Nathan. He talked with the other men and Murphy stood by his side. Without looking, Nathan's hand found her coat, playfully patting her above the collar. Murphy felt calm and happy. There was nowhere else she'd rather be.

The group continued to make its long, slow crawl toward camp. The crisp fall air was a reminder that it would be their last mountain adventure of the season.

They continued to caravan single file, winding over rocks, maneuvering their vehicles at impossible angles. The boys cheered when their bodies turned sideways, loving it, remembering the first, terrifying time they had gone off-roading. Now, having to navigate the trail in the darkness because they got a late start, the exhilaration intensified. Who needed expensive thrills at an amusement park when they could get this?

Once they arrived at camp the sound of gurgling water in the not-so-far-away distance was the only thing they could hear. While everyone else had to rely on flashlights, Murphy's nighttime vision allowed her to go to the sound. She quickly explored before finding the water source, a little creek adjacent to camp; a run-off from the reservoir. Murphy lapped greedily at the cold water, enjoying the cool sensation on her nose and jowls.

The group enjoyed working for the simple conveniences most people take for granted every day—a roof, a warm place to sleep, and food. As they pitched the tents, they talked and laughed. Not one head was looking at any sort of technological device.

The kids toyed with their tent as the fathers expertly pitched their own one-man dwellings around the perimeter. They teased about who should be the farthest away, in order to banish the snorers, and Nathan gave Matthew and Joey a reminder not to leave food in their tents.

"It'll bring the bears out," he said, the boys' eyes wide as they listened. "And don't pee right by your tent, either. That'll attract 'em too."

As usual, they planned to cook their meals over a fire that weekend. When they would settle in to eat the food they had prepared, whether it was hot dogs, pancakes, or eggs and bacon, Matthew always thought their simple camping food tasted better than anything they could have cooked at home. And whether it was night or day, none of the boys or men ever got tired of looking up at the massive sky or breathing in the clear, mountain air.

As much as they all liked the break from the fast-paced outside world, and nothing was amiss except for the quick hiccup back at Worton's, they would soon discover that this particular trip would be different from the countless carefree ones they'd taken so many times before. This would be the one time they would yearn for modern, technological advancements, particularly communication with the outside world. Nathan didn't know it, but he would especially come to wish that someone, anyone, could hear them.

Chapter 6

The next morning the clear daylight illuminated where water had once flowed, but had evaporated during the drought. There was a water line that stopped at the edge of the bleached white rocks and on the other side of it, a thick forest of shrubs and pine trees grew. It was the first time the friends had been to this campsite at 6,000 feet elevation. They were where the Rubicon River, an offshoot of the mighty American River, flows into Hell Hole Reservoir, but there wasn't a drop of water to be seen. Legend has it that the name Hell Hole came from pioneers looking for gold in the region. The nickname is easy to imagine. As one pioneer struggled to climb up out of the reservoir's basin he turned to another gold seeker and asked, "This is one hell of a hole, ain't it?"

Even 170 years later, no one can argue the canyon at Hell Hole's foundation isn't deep.

There hadn't been much rain in California during the previous few years; 2012 was officially the beginning of a drought that would last four years.

Normally the flow of water from the Rubicon River to Hell Hole flows like an artery, unseen. But now it was just a trickle. If you peered closely into the reservoir's basin you could see that it was as dry as a scrubbed sink. Because of its long shape, it actually looked more like a bathtub. While Hell Hole is large enough to hold enough water for boats and other water sports, Matthew and Joey wouldn't be swimming this time. Instead white boulders, bleached by the sun over generations, lay exposed where water should have been, spanning as far as the eye could see.

The wide open space attracted target shooters because it was the perfect spot to see clearly for miles, the perfect place to practice a centered, bulls-eye shot. Murphy trotted alongside the group. A thin, chalky substance covered her paws—the remains of countless clay objects other campers had shot during target practice.

"It looks like we're on the moon," Matthew said, staring at the expanse of white.

As the boys kicked sand and shale at the bottom of the reservoir, Joey looked ahead, beyond a few straggler trees and asked, "Can we walk down to the river?"

"You won't find much there," Nathan answered, taking a sip from a water bottle. "It's probably dried up, too."

The Rubicon River, a once mighty body of water, had become as timid as a backyard creek.

Chapter 7

Two hunters fired up at a cluster of squirrels. One fell from a tree limb to the ground. The other two were lucky; they scurried up the tree and got away.

"Got it," Riam said.

"That was mine," his brother, Chu Cai, replied with a smile. The brothers' only physical similarity was the same coloring—they had the same short black hair and golden skin tone, but Riam was tall and lanky while Cai was shorter and heavier set. Riam casually strode over, picked up the lifeless creature by the tail, and tossed it into a burlap sack the size of a pillowcase.

Behind them, 12-year-old Paj watched her father and uncle banter, and she thought it was funny. *It doesn't matter when brothers and sisters grow up, they still compete*, she thought.

"How many did you catch today?" Paj asked as

her father and uncle turned back toward camp. "Five?"

"Four," Riam replied flatly.

Paj's mouth was as dry as sandpaper. She had finished all her water while watching the men hunt. Paj was small and thin. She pulled back her long black hair with both hands, collecting it at her neck before she began twisting it into a bun. She had nothing to tie her locks with, so as soon as she let go her mane cascaded around her slight shoulders.

"Save some water for later," her father had said. He had been right. Her stomach began to rumble, too.

"That took a long time," Paj told the men, scratching her cheek, her amusement fading.

"Squirrels are hard to catch in these mountains," Father told her, folding the sack shut as he spoke. "They are not like the friendly squirrels you see in the park."

Paj imagined kids tossing their snacks to the squirrels back home in Sacramento and how those squirrels would come right up close to people to get the easy offerings, protectively clutching them close.

"Up here you have to walk quietly or the squirrels run away," father said matter-of-factly.

Paj usually stayed with the women back at camp, but this time she wanted to see what the men did while they were away all day. She left with her father and Chu Cai while her mother and aunties stayed back with the younger children.

"What is so great that you want to come up to the mountains all the time?" Paj had asked.

Her father tousled her hair and said, "Come see."

Chapter 8

At lunchtime on their first full day, Murphy wagged her tail and begged with her eyes every time Nathan took a hot dog from the campfire grill, slid it into a bun, and held it out for one of the campers to take. She got up from her polite seated position and, nose twitching, moved closer and closer to Nathan, giving him the look that didn't always successfully lead to him giving her food when they were back at home in El Dorado Hills.

"How can I say no to you, Murph?" Nathan laughed and stooped down to offer Murphy a plain link without a bun.

Tail wagging, Murphy gladly accepted the treasure, cradling it in her mouth as she trotted off to a corner of the campsite to enjoy the salty, warm treat.

Life was good and food had always come easy to Murphy. She'd had a pleasant beginning with the other puppies in her litter and transitioned smoothly to a life of luxury by dog standards, ever since the Braun family adopted her.

On these off-roading camping trips some things were certain; rules softened for the kids, and as an extension of the children, rules went by the wayside for Murphy too. No one handed her hot dogs for any good reason at home, where one was to be had only if it accidentally slipped from the baby, Finegan's, grasp. Or, what was more likely, Finegan made a game of it in the way toddlers do. He often let bits of scrambled egg or whole pieces of bread tumble from his highchair tray, even pushing them off of the ledge on purpose. Murphy knew to wait patiently next to the highchair just in case, and the chances were good that she would be rewarded for her patience.

Finegan definitely gave Murphy the most food, but it is an unfortunate fact of dog life that scraps come less frequently as children grow older. And all dogs know that once the masters lower their voices, the fun is about to be ruined. Murphy would stand there sheepishly once Erin and Nathan began to talk in a stern way to the children about why dogs shouldn't eat any of the varieties of food people get to enjoy every day. This was silly to Murphy because all foods were delicious to her.

Once the kids got specific, asking if they could give Murphy this treat or that, the parents would predictably say, "Dog food is just fine for her." Or, which is always the clincher, "It'll make her sick." Murphy couldn't understand all of the words, but she knew the tones of their voices meant the fun was over and the looks on their faces, brows furrowed, said it too.

When the Braun kids would ask, "Why not?" Erin and Nathan would point to Murphy, who would inevitably be standing a little too close to the table, ready to grab, and say something about creating a "poorly behaved" or "begging dog."

Murphy didn't agree, not in the least. The crackers, cereal, and bits of shredded chicken Finegan dropped were delicious and never made Murphy anything but hungry for more.

In times like these, Murphy was left to begrudgingly eat one, predictably boring thing— kibble.

As Murphy enjoyed her hot dog in the fresh mountain air, it was clear—camping is fun for everyone.

Chapter 9

Target shooting was one of the guys' regular camping activities and it wasn't new to Murphy, either. She had joined Nathan on plenty of camping trips over the years. Early that afternoon, Matthew and Joey settled in to watch the men get ready for target practice. The boys' faces were dirty from lunch, sticky with ketchup and root beer, but happy.

One might think that target practice and color blindness wouldn't go together, or that color blindness would be a disadvantage during such an activity, but that wasn't the case for Nathan's friend, Bubba.

Like one in 10 American men Bubba couldn't see red or green the way most people do; gray and blue looked brown to him. Bubba liked to joke that color blindness was actually his superpower and he constantly reminded his friends that color blind men were coveted as soldiers in World War II for their ability to easily spot the enemy's camouflage. That didn't mean his friends didn't tease him about it, especially when Bubba would say his famous phrase, "I'll find it." Those words would actually become proof of his superpower.

Once his friends and family began to realize he was serious, the teasing stopped, because Bubba always found whatever "it" was. One time he crawled under Nathan and Erin's backyard deck to search for a diamond necklace that had slipped through a crack.

Everyone was searching for it, down on their hands and knees with flashlights when Bubba announced, "I'll find it," and disappeared from sight.

In less than two minutes Bubba reappeared, a smile brighter than the gems he held in the air. He had literally found a diamond in the rough.

Instead of shooting at cans for practice, this time they brought fluorescent orange disks that they tossed in the air with a special stick called a chucker. They aimed their guns to shoot the disks in the air before they fell to the ground. The diameter of a flattened baseball, the disks are also called pigeons because of how they fly through the air.

At the sound of the first shot, Murphy stopped exploring and stood at attention.

The blasts kept coming. Soon the men tossed more disks in the air. They started to feel competitive because of Bubba's advantage. The orange disk stood out brighter for him; he could see its three dimensions better than anyone else could.

Bubba continued to be a perfect shot.

The men were paying close attention to their sport. The pace picked up as Bubba kept hitting the target. Excitement filled the air as the pellets whizzed through it, exploding the targets one by one.

"Shoot three at a time!" someone challenged, fueling a live drama that was, in fact, the first of its kind for Murphy.

Matthew and Joey wore earmuffs and smiles.

Murphy's heartbeat jumped and she began to zip around, dodging back and forth, as a pleading, frantic whine built up, growing stronger with every shot.

"Shhh," Matthew said, reaching for Murphy, massaging her back and neck. Murphy couldn't be still, though. She walked a short distance away from the group but continued to pace. All eyes were on the action the dads were creating, but Murphy's ears were desperate for peace.

Soon four disks were in the air at once.

Murphy circled until she was about to burst. *Please stop!* her eyes begged and her tail demanded.

When Nathan looked back in the bright afternoon sun, he noticed that the kids were there, but Murphy wasn't. Little did he know that Murphy had just run into the forest, her amber fur a dazzling streak that zoomed by as fast and suddenly as one of the flying pellets.

Chapter 10

Nathan played the last moments he saw Murphy over and over in his mind. They'd thrown countless targets in the air before realizing Murphy had fled the scene. As soon as they realized she wasn't there, the laughter abruptly stopped and everyone started calling for her.

Nathan looked everywhere he could see in the vast, white, wide open space.

He placed his shotgun back in its locked case and turned his body in every direction to look for any sign of Murphy. It would be easy to see her golden coat if she were near.

"Come here, girl," he called at first, raising his voice louder in his growing anxiety.

Matthew was confused.

"The loud blasts must have scared her," Nathan

reassured him. "She'll be back...just wait."

Nathan's words, and the hope that they would be true, lifted his own spirits.

In the matter of one hour, Nathan's feelings would change many times. He went from frustrated to disbelieving and then to being very worried about Murphy. At the slightest sound, Nathan and Matthew would turn, their chests exhaling with relief, expecting to see Murphy back with them, panting, eyes ablaze, happy to be with her family.

But every time they heard a noise it wasn't Murphy.

As hours passed, Nathan's feelings morphed into feelings of guilt. Murphy had gone hunting with him since she was a pup and was used to the noise that firearms make. This time, they'd gotten out of hand trying to challenge Bubba and showing off their skills.

The group searched as far as they could see. Once the sun set, Nathan put on his headlamp to search the rest of the canyon, a small speck compared to the forest, which is one million acres; about the size of the state of Rhode Island.

"Murph, come here girl!" Nathan called for what seemed like the millionth time.

He decided to search alone. The four men felt young at heart whenever they were together, but age can be fickle. They weren't as strong as they once were, even if they still felt like they were in their twenties.

His friends got up to join him as soon as Nathan

started to tie the laces of his hiking boots. He worried about Matthew and Joey trying to make the trek, too.

"Why don't you guys stay here in case Murphy comes back to camp?" Nathan said to the group as he positioned his backpack.

He headed into the thick brush of expansive forest that circled the empty reservoir. The thought of Murphy returning while he was out sustained Nathan, but when he looked at his phone to see if there was any news from back at camp, the screen kept reflecting the same annoying message—NO SERVICE.

Chapter 11

Nathan walked through the forest all night and into the early morning wearing only jeans and a sweatshirt, a headlamp offering the only light. The lightbulb seemed dimmer than before and Nathan was concerned that the batteries might die. To conserve it, he'd turn the lamp off when he'd stop to rest, his breathing the only sound he could hear. When he'd resume walking, Nathan took comfort in the twigs that crunched beneath his boots, each marking another step in his search, one step closer to finding Murphy, who must be cold and tired by then.

Many times Nathan's mind went to Murphy's collar. If someone found her, they'd find the family's address and phone number and they would call.

As the sun began to rise in the early morning dawn, Nathan turned off his headlamp for good. His feet were sore but his heart and mind were resolute. He wouldn't give up until he found Murphy.

Maybe someone has already called, Nathan thought and would instinctively look at his phone, only to see the same lonely message—NO SERVICE.

When Nathan looped back and saw their campsite from a distance, he was surprised to see a campfire already blazing. He squinted to see if he could see Murphy, but as he came closer he only saw the bright orange flame of the fire. He was greeted by the men drinking coffee and warming their hands, but before Nathan even had a chance to ask, their eyes told him that Murphy had not returned.

"Wait until full daylight," one of the men said. "We'll find her."

Nathan dreaded telling Erin that Murphy was gone. Saying the words out loud would make everything real. Still, he knew what he needed to do.

He walked toward the dry canyon, where the Rubicon once flowed mightily, and suddenly, thankfully, there was a slight cell signal. Instead of NO SERVICE one bar appeared on his phone.

It's a miracle! Nathan thought, taking some comfort in the small gift.

He didn't want to call home so early. He knew that Erin would be worried by the phone ringing that early in the morning, not to mention he was dreading to share the upsetting news. Still, Nathan knew that honesty was at the core of his and Erin's relationship and he'd certainly want Erin to do the same if she were ever in his situation. Their 15-year marriage was strong because it was based on friendship. They endured things most married couples don't experience early on and their shared losses bonded them as tight as glue. First Nathan's father died. Not long after, Erin's mother passed away, and then seven months later her father died too; they would never know any of Erin's three children.

She had been raised in the Bay Area, in a happy home with two parents who loved her. Like Nathan, she was also the youngest of four children, but her circumstances were a bit different. Erin had been adopted when she was only a few days old.

Her parents each had health issues and had decided not to create children of their own, but still wanted a full house of children. So they adopted Erin and her three older siblings, all from different birth mothers in California, during the mid-to-late 1960s.

Love still couldn't save Erin's parents from their health woes, however. Though they died within months of each other, leaving a devastating void, the love they raised their children with was not in vain. Erin and Nathan wanted to create a big family together and it gave them comfort to do so. It was to carry on their parents' legacies and, in a small way, softened the heartbreak of losing them.

Nathan and Erin grew up in the same region of the Bay Area. It wasn't until they began dating in their twenties that they realized they had attended the same Catholic grammar school in San Jose. Nathan's mother even had proof that Nathan and Erin had met years before as children, when they attended the same private school. For years Nathan's mother, Carmen, held a long-forgotten letter Erin had written to her future husband when they were little children. When Nathan was in second grade and Erin was in sixth grade, her class acted as a "big buddy" class to Nathan's, penning letters of encouragement to one another. Later they even recalled that Erin had played volleyball with Nathan's sister at that school. At Erin's bridal shower, Carmen presented Erin with the letter. Who would have ever guessed that one day that little letter writer would become Nathan's bride?

When the phone rang back at home in El Dorado Hills, it woke Erin out of a peaceful sleep. An automatic sinking feeling washed over her—the dread when a phone rings too early in the morning or too late at night.

It's someone calling with news that can't wait, she thought.

"Hi," Erin said, when she saw it was Nathan. Her blond hair was tousled and her green eyes were bright as she propped herself up to a half-seated position.

Nathan swallowed before speaking and figured he may as well get to the point. "Murphy's missing," he said.

No coffee needed. Erin sat straight up, fully awake.

"What?" she asked. "What happened?"

"She's been gone since yesterday. The target

shooting must've scared her off," Nathan said.

His voice trailed off. Then, "I thought for sure she would've come back last night…"

Erin's first thought was, *Murphy can't survive in the wild*…

Then, *If she's still alive, she won't be for long.*

The more Nathan talked, the more Erin could tell how upset he was. She felt compassion for her husband, but didn't know what to do with the news. Her mind raced to thoughts of Murphy all alone, fending for herself in the wild.

Just as suddenly, an image of the survival instincts Erin knew Murphy possessed flooded over Erin, and she felt hopeful. Hope in that moment was a small gift that loosened the chain of fear that had so suddenly gripped her insides.

Chapter 12

Though the Brauns always had golden retrievers, usually two at a time to keep each other company, Murphy stood out as a hunter like no other dog they'd had before. She chased the squirrels that effortlessly tight-roped along the top of their backyard fence. Murphy would run back and forth, her eyes never moving away from the quick, brown dashes that flitted by in an instant. If one of the squirrels ever did end up on the grass, Murphy was sure to capture it.

Once, Murphy came to the back door, a lifeless squirrel hanging from her mouth, full of pride because of the best present she could offer her family. Before long a new squirrel would begin to frequent their yard, and a new round of the same chasing game soon followed.

Another time Murphy brought a baby chipmunk into the house and dropped it on the kitchen floor as if to say, "Look what I got you!"

Yet this time the creature wasn't lifeless; it was very much alive. The startled chipmunk wasn't as amused as Murphy was in that moment. She held the frightened little rodent in her mouth, shaking it back and forth like a salt shaker. "EEEKK!" the helpless prey squealed.

"Drop it," Erin said, expecting the chipmunk to be still after such a thrashing, but it stood and scurried to the fence.

Nathan gingerly rescued the little animal, scooping it up with a shovel. *Saved for another day,* he thought before pressing it through a hole in one of the slats of their fence. The little chipmunk was given its freedom, but for how long was anyone's guess. Murphy resumed looking for it immediately.

Another time Murphy was successful in a seemingly impossible feat when she caught a fly in her mouth while they were at the river. Before the victory, Murphy's eyes had been following the fly, back and forth like a pendulum, while her body stood perfectly still, at attention. Once the fly came within reach Murphy coolly snapped her jaw in the air, a quick open and shut, and in an instant the buzzing stopped. To everyone's astonishment, she'd gotten it.

Back at home, Erin said goodbye to Nathan. When she put down the phone, she was certain Murphy was still alive. Another feeling that was just as strong washed over her too—that they were in a race against time to make sure Murphy stayed alive. They had to get to her, and quickly. As worried as Erin was about Murphy, she was worried about Nathan too and knew he would push himself to his physical limits in the search.

Erin knew who she needed to call next.

Larry was another friend in their tight-knit group. He was a single father who came across as a tough guy and sometimes used words that would make people blush. Despite the tough exterior, Larry had a soft side and a heart of gold. Larry hadn't gone on the camping trip because he had to work that weekend, but when he got the call from Erin that Murphy was lost, and that his four buddies were running out of energy to find her, he drove three hours and hiked the Rubicon on foot to meet up with his friends and help with the search. That's just the kind of friend Larry was.

Chapter 13

Nathan cancelled his work trip and stayed an extra night with Larry and Bubba, scouring the reservoir and campground for miles. Joey's dad Brian brought the boys home on Sunday night to get them home for school.

If the ride to get down the trail was an adventure, the slow ride back without Murphy was just plain long. They twisted over rocks, maneuvering their vehicles at impossible angles, but instead of cheering when their bodies turned sideways as before, this time Matthew and Joey remained quiet. Like a balloon that's lost its air, the celebratory mood deflated right along with Murphy's disappearance.

The exhaustion from the past 24-hour search was evident in the dusting of dirt smudged across Matthew's cheek. Deep in sleep, Matthew's chest rose and fell with each breath. Nathan would be grateful to hear that at long last his son had succumbed to sleep after tossing and turning in his tent all night. Nathan knew that none of them would get much sleep in the coming days.

Once Nathan forced himself to leave in the morning, eyes tired and feet sore, he felt irritable and impatient on the long, slow journey home. Each minute, and each mile, separated him from Murphy even more. He couldn't believe Murphy hadn't come back and that he was actually leaving without her.

One thought ran through Nathan's mind during the long trip back up the Rubicon Trail—*I left home with three members of my family and now only two are returning.*

The guilt made his stomach ache and a choking throb clutched his throat.

Just as Hansel and Gretel had left a bread crumb trail in order to find their way back home, Nathan threw dog kibble out of his Jeep as he winded slowly back up and over each rock, hopeful that the clues would somehow help Murphy find her way back to their family. Nathan's mind crowded with a stream of ideas he could use to get Murphy home safe and sound.

As he stared at the road, Nathan planned to go home long enough to regroup and get some clean clothes before heading back down the Rubicon to search for Murphy.

Chapter 14

A first generation American, Paj came from a long line of Hmong (pronounced "Mung") hunters. A culture of people originally from the mountain regions in China, Laos, Thailand, and Vietnam, there are more Hmong immigrants in the Sacramento area than almost any other city in the United States, second only to Minneapolis. With its cool winters and hot summers, Hmong immigrants choose Sacramento to settle down and build new lives because the nearby Sierra Nevada Mountain range is a lot like home.

Because it is a part of Hmong culture to hunt for food, many families travel to the high Sierra every summer and fall to find their own food and the grand prize is a bear, which is especially sought for its gallbladder, known as a delicacy.

This was the third weekend in a row that Paj, her

parents, and extended family packed up their simple camping gear and drove to the mountains, trying to get their last bounty before the animals went into hibernation. Paj and her mother sat alongside Paj's father, Riam, in their tan pickup truck as Riam sped along the bumpy Rubicon Trail.

While bear hunting was a favorite tradition in her family, Paj was the first one in her family who didn't seem to have the love of hunting inside her. Her father and uncle still held out hope that they might change that.

Capturing a bear may be a prize, mostly because of the rarity of being able to do so. Riam might catch one a season, if he were lucky. Even if he didn't, their countless trips to the forest weren't in vain. Riam and the other hunters also enjoyed the more common squirrel meat, so when they caught a few dozen squirrels on these hunting trips it was an added bonus.

Her parents and grandparents had made it an annual tradition to stock up on squirrel meat from late fall through early winter. Squirrels provided the main ingredient for camp dinners and the leftovers were taken back home. Paj's parents and older relatives especially enjoyed squirrel stew in cold weather.

For Riam and his brothers, hunting was a way to provide for their families. It's easy to go to the store, but through patience and skill they were able to give nourishment to their wives and children, and that felt good. Hunting was also an opportunity to relax and spend time doing an activity they enjoyed together.

It was indeed a celebration if one of them got a bear, but it was almost certain that Riam would bring a bag of fresh squirrels back to camp. And when he did, Paj's mother, Anh, would unwrap the bag and pull out the squirrels like they were potatoes. She'd deftly cut the head and tail off of one and save the others for later. Added to vegetables and hot, steaming broth, one squirrel was the perfect amount for a pot of stew.

Paj enjoyed their fall camping trips for many reasons, but the squirrel stew was not one of them. It was okay, but she would rather eat American foods like hamburgers and waffles, which she didn't get to enjoy very often. When the other kids at school bought school lunches from the cafeteria and returned to the long tables with their trays, complaining about "too much grease" on their pizza or "cold" chicken nuggets, Paj thought their food looked delicious.

It wasn't that she was ever hungry. In fact, Paj probably had the freshest food, which took the most care in preparing. Her parents packed her lunch every day; things like shrimp, noodles, and vegetables. But the other children teased her for the foods' unusual containers and smells.

When she opened her homemade lunch and her classmates wrinkled their noses and said, "Ewwww! What's that?" Paj wanted to say, "It's no less tasty, just different." Instead, she put her head down and her cheeks burned red with shame.

As they walked back to camp Paj looked at her father, stifling a giggle. He looked like a much skinnier Santa Claus with a small sack of presents slung over his shoulder. Not unlike Santa Claus, Riam and Chu Cai's treasures were gifts that made them feel joy and pride when giving them.

Chapter 15

Riam had come to America with his parents and two brothers when he was a boy in the early 1980s.

Neither he nor Anh had gone to college; they were too busy working to put food on the table. Despite this, by the time their only child was born they realized that a good education allows for the most opportunities, and so a college education became the biggest dream they had for their daughter. They hoped Paj would become a doctor, a lawyer, a dentist, or an engineer. To them, those professions spelled success. In seeing their child become successful, they would see their own American dream fulfilled.

The American dream was extended to just about everything in their adopted homeland.

"Only in America…" they liked to say, before delving into the many reasons they loved the Land of Liberty.

"Only in America, the grocery store aisles are filled with food...one whole section with cereal alone," her father told her.

Or, "Only in America, an immigrant's daughter can become a doctor one day, or even the President of the United States," Anh reminded her.

The one conflict between what they wanted and what could be a reality came down to education. Paj heard what they said about its importance, and tried her best in school, but she felt confused sometimes. Her father always said she must go to school so she would not end up like him, but Paj didn't know anyone in her life as kind or as smart as her father.

After working long hours as a custodian Riam wanted to talk with Paj about her school day, and he always asked to look at her math homework. Those were her favorite moments; she savored any time she got to spend with her hardworking father.

The only time Paj became unhappy with her father was when he didn't let her do things the other kids at her school did, like go to the mall or listen to popular music. After school Paj wanted to shop at stores like Justice and Tilly's. Her mouth watered when she thought of buying pizza or gelato at a food court and she imagined what it would be like to call home on a cell phone when she was ready to be picked up.

Instead, she'd wait for her dad at the shopping center where he worked. His to-do list was never ending. He'd take out the trash, vacuum, and clean the restrooms in the various businesses at the center, only to have to start all over again at night when the shops and small businesses were empty. When everyone else went home to have dinner with their families, Riam was just getting started.

"Honest work," he would say to his daughter. "My father was a doctor in Vietnam, but in America he was a janitor, too."

Either Riam or Anh always added, "You can be a doctor in America."

Paj tried to do well in school, but she had to put in more effort than most kids she knew. When she was younger, Paj saw how other parents came to help in the classroom. They'd sit and read to their sons and daughters in the library as if they had all the time in the world. When they weren't working or doing chores at home, Riam and Anh preferred to listen to their American daughter read to them, instead.

Paj's parents always seemed to be working. When they were at home there wasn't time to relax on the couch or watch television, but when she was near, Riam always included Paj in whatever chore he was doing so they could spend time together. They were very close and Paj knew that if Riam was ever upset with her, it was because he was more hurt than angry.

Her relationship with her mother wasn't as easy. Since she'd started middle school, Paj and her mother had begun to argue more. Paj often bit her lip when she wanted to talk back or ask "why" about something. Sometimes she couldn't help it, and words escaped her mouth that surprised even her. Even so, she didn't say a quarter of what she really felt to her mother and so was surprised whenever she heard kids her age speaking disrespectfully to their parents. For the most part Paj remained quiet, but that didn't mean she wasn't fuming.

Paj's mother worked long hours at a nail salon, hunched over all day, clipping nails and rubbing feet until her hands were pruned and her back ached. When she got home Anh cooked lunch and dinner for the next day and somehow still kept their home in meticulous order.

She was less tender than Riam, often shouting orders at Paj, but she was only doing what she'd known. Anh's own mother had been the same way with her.

Whenever Paj felt as if an ocean separated her from her mother, she liked to remember when her mom used to braid her hair. Mother's hands, strong yet delicate, worked through Paj's hair and the steady tugging felt good. Even though she would be too embarrassed to wear her hair that way now, Paj longed for that closeness with her mother.

"You'll be a failure if you don't work hard in school," Anh would say, but when she brushed Paj's hair or handed her a steaming plate of food, Paj saw love and softness in her mother's eyes.

Paj thought that out of all the other parents she knew, hers were the most vocal about "a good education." What made Paj struggle was how hard "a good education" is, certainly much harder than it sounds.

Paj thought about a bully at school then, and her cheeks flushed hot with a memory from just that morning.

"What did you get on your vocab test?" the boy had asked.

Paj's stomach clenched when she thought about the look on his face, those teasing eyes, his mouth turned up in a mocking grin. He knew very well what score she'd gotten on the test but asked anyway, looking at her paper as she tried to hide it from his view. A red 10/20 was boldly written at the top.

Despite their scolding, Paj's family didn't make her feel small in this way. She liked hearing their stories, especially when her father told her about his childhood in Vietnam. Paj never tired of hearing about when Riam came to America and how stores were the biggest difference, and shock, to him, with all those stocked shelves and endless choices.

The next biggest surprise to Riam was to see so many people with a silver gate attached to their teeth—braces. It took him a while to figure out that they were actually straightening people's teeth. He was used to crooked teeth being as normal as seeing two eyes and a nose on someone's face. Once he realized what they were used for, he got quite a laugh!

Paj was an American girl. Grocery stores and braces were normal to her, but sometimes, like at school, her family's differences made her feel left out, making her believe she wasn't really sure where she belonged. Sometimes she didn't feel like she belonged at home either, but at least at home she knew she was loved.

They were nearly back to camp. The sun was lowering in the sky. Paj figured her mother and aunts would be peeling vegetables for dinner about then. If she were there, she would be responsible for watching her younger cousins. She wondered how the women were managing without her.

A scuffle back at camp brought Paj back to the present. She heard her mother's voice rise.

"Shoo," she snapped. "There's nothing here for you."

Chapter 16

Paj saw something golden standing next to the iron pot over the fire.

A coyote or a mountain lion, she thought, and a feeling of dread consumed her.

She stood back until the animal turned and began to walk away from Anh, who waited, hands on her hips. When it looked back, Paj could tell it was harmless; just a very dirty, frail looking, and most likely very hungry, golden retriever.

Paj walked toward the dog, wary to find one in such a remote location all by itself. Not sure if the animal would bite, Paj stood back to be sure. The dog looked at her, its eyes happy but tired. Paj reached her fist out and the dog came right to her, tail wagging.

Paj instinctively went to pet her new friend and felt burrs in every inch of its tangled coat. Paj gingerly began twisting the prickly pests out, not sure if she was hurting the animal. Instead she was greeted with happy eyes and a wagging tail. Paj continued to wind each spiky object out, one by one, tossing each into the brush. She gently rubbed the dog's head and looked into its eyes.

Paj reached for something on the dog's neck—a brown leather collar. She fumbled for a name tag or for anything that might solve the mystery as to whom the dog belonged. She looked side to side, as though the dog's rightful owner might show up at any moment. It was so late in the season, and there had not been any other campers at the campsite. Paj didn't expect to see any newcomers now.

Maybe someone new has arrived, Paj thought, but she didn't see any other cars besides their tan pickup truck and her uncle's red one. He'd come with his family the day before to get a head start.

Paj read the two addresses and two phone numbers listed on the dog's tag. One was in El Dorado Hills, which she had heard mentioned before. She was pretty sure it was near her home in Sacramento. The other address on the tag was in Lake Tahoe.

A tag means it has a home, Paj thought. *But if the dog has a collar, why is it looking for food? Why is it all alone and so dirty? Where is its owner?*

Paj continued to peer at the little piece of metal around the dog's neck as though deciphering a mystery code. "Murphy," she mouthed silently, then whispered, "Murphy."

The dog began to wag its tail even harder upon hearing her name.

"Murphy Braun," Paj read to herself, mouthing the words.

With a name like Murphy, it never occurred to Paj that her new friend could be female.

Murphy is a boy's name, she thought.

Paj smiled and cuddled Murphy close. Paj had always wanted a dog of her very own, but her parents didn't think of dogs as pets to love, but as beings to hunt or work for them. They'd said no plenty of times when she'd asked for a pet in the past.

Paj looked at Murphy who was looking up at her, panting, tail wagging, with all those burrs stuck to her coat.

Paj knew deep down in her gut that her parents would certainly say no to this grimy golden retriever too.

She stood a little taller with the thought that she might be able to persuade them. She suddenly knew what she could say to her mother and father, something that might give her a sliver of a chance to let Murphy stay with them.

Murphy looked at Paj, continuing to whip her tail back and forth, so happy not to be alone any longer.

Chapter 17

Paj watched her father place his shotgun in the back of his truck, and then turn to walk toward Anh with the sack of squirrels slung over his shoulder. He swung it gently around and handed it to her by the makeshift chef's workspace which she had created by the campsite's fire pit and picnic table.

Anh's eyes turned toward her daughter, paying no mind to, or at least not noticing, the animal beside her.

She skillfully prepared one squirrel. "You hungry?" Anh asked in Vietnamese. She stood at the large pot over the fire, the air hazy, floating above it, and held the skinned squirrel to the water's boiling surface before plopping it in.

"Yes," Paj replied in English.

Her mother bustled over to the table to fix Paj

some sticky rice and vegetables, as comfortable in the simple, outdoor camping kitchen as in their kitchen back at home.

Murphy sniffed the air. Pasty spittle began to form at the corners of her mouth. It would have been drool, but she hadn't had enough water since she'd been fending for herself out in the woods.

Paj walked to the spigot to wash her hands. The water was cold, but felt good. Murphy got up and stood by her side, slurping the water that ran off and caught in the grate.

I'm not letting this friend out of my sight, Murphy thought as the cool water soothed her insides.

Anh took notice and eyed Murphy disapprovingly.

Like deflecting a blow, Paj moved out of the way.

"Come," she called to her new companion, walking away from her mother, and settling beneath a nearby tree. Murphy gladly came toward her. The pain Murphy felt in her paws from days of walking and the ache on her left side from a burr that still poked into her skin were nearly forgotten, as she savored the sweet moment of companionship.

Paj ate quickly. The food was warm and settled comfortably in her empty belly. Murphy sat by the girl's side, panting, looking at the bowl and then back at Paj. Little did Paj know how famished Murphy was. Still, as before, Murphy's hunger was less intense, but never entirely forgotten, because she had company.

Paj dropped some rice and a snow pea on the ground. Murphy ate it in one bite and then looked at

Paj for more. The smells all around her, from the food Paj ate and the squirrels boiling over the fire, soothed Murphy.

Paj moved the bowl closer to Murphy. "Go ahead," she said.

Murphy waited.

Paj tapped the bowl and said it again. "Eat."

Murphy leaned over and dug her nose into the smallish dish, her hesitance forgotten and her loneliness all but forgotten, too.

Once Murphy ate that bowl of food, Paj quietly scooped in some more for her. Fatigue settling in from having her stomach full for the first time in nearly a week, Murphy rested.

Paj remembered the collar. She reached for it and found even more burrs embedded in Murphy's fur around the edges. She also noticed that the white of Murphy's left eye was pink. Paj gently felt around the edge of the eye and pulled one of the thorny objects from the fur.

Murphy licked her hand. Paj giggled.

Paj loosened the collar, but once she felt more rough edges, she wanted to release poor Murphy from any thorns that might be pressing down with the collar. Murphy panted as she looked at Paj.

I think you're wonderful, Murphy's eyes smiled as she looked gratefully at her new companion, wagging her tail so hard that her body swayed.

Paj unbuckled the collar and removed it from around the dog's neck. The fur underneath the collar was very clean, compared to the fur that surrounded it. Paj combed the dirty, matted coat with her fingers, blending it with the hair that had been pressed flat by the collar. It felt so good to Murphy.

Suddenly Paj stopped. She had an idea. She knew how she might ensure Murphy could go home with her!

"What are you doing?" Anh asked, walking toward the two new friends, interrupting Paj's thoughts. "Why did you give that dog your bowl?"

"He's hungry," Paj answered, still unaware Murphy was actually female.

Silence. Anh sighed and leaned down to retrieve something from inside a tent.

Paj hid the collar so that her mother wouldn't learn that Murphy, indeed, already had a home.

Murphy is starving and as thirsty as someone stranded in a desert, Paj thought, justifying in her mind the action she planned to take next.

Murphy is practically dying of thirst. She's drained bowls of water and I haven't seen her pee once, Paj continued, building a strong case in her mind.

One thought consumed Paj, filling her with energy.

I know what I need to do to save Murphy! She screamed in her mind.

To think Murphy might possibly become her very own pet, a pet to love and who wouldn't judge her, was thrilling. Paj's heart raced because deep down she knew it was wrong to lie and sneak, but the

77

temptation was too strong and her bond to the stray dog too quick.

She walked to the nearest trash bin and dumped the collar, and with it the only identifying mark that Murphy had ever belonged to anyone else.

Chapter 18

Paj's mother emerged from the tent and walked over to Murphy to make a closer inspection.

Murphy panted, happy to have anyone near her. Yet in the way Anh carried herself, Murphy sensed this woman was a leader and so she rolled on her back, leaving her belly up in a defenseless position.

Anh wasn't swayed or softened. "This dog is a she, not he," Anh said matter-of-factly as she peered at Murphy, cocking her head sideways for a closer look.

Murphy? Paj thought about the name. *What kind of a girl name is that?*

"Can we keep her?" Paj asked her mother, much more concerned about the dog's future than whether she was male or female.

Anh hesitated, and to Paj the weight of the world

was in her impending answer.

"While camping, yes. At home, no," Anh replied.

Paj's stomach hurtled down as though she were falling. She couldn't say she was surprised, but her mother's words were still a blow.

When Paj's mother was a girl in Vietnam she had learned at a young age, much younger than Paj was, that the animals in her life weren't for companionship, as American pets are thought to be. In Vietnam animals were meant to provide safety or food. Her family's watch dogs stayed outside and guarded their crops from intruders.

Once when Anh's father brought home three chickens for their steady egg supply, seven-year-old Anh never thought to name them, as children in America might. Instead of providing eggs for the family, the chickens had started eating their own eggs. Anh's father knew what this meant. So, one by one, the chickens were the main courses at dinner within the week.

Before then, the closest Anh ever came to feeling attached to an animal was when a wild boar roamed onto their land looking for food. Anh had been five or six at that time. She had found the boar and tried to hide it, just as Paj was trying to hide Murphy. With delight, she began to romp around with the boar, but her father saw it and butchered it for its meat by the end of that day.

The memory came back to Anh as she saw her daughter's hopeful expression with Murphy at her side. She remembered what it was like to be the same age as Paj, and in that moment Anh's heart softened.

"She can keep guard for us tonight," Anh offered, her eyes downcast as she turned back to stir the stew.

"Thank you," Paj said, grateful for this gesture. With this bit of hope, Paj believed that a guard dog could turn into a pet of her very own.

They will see how much we need Murphy, she thought.

Paj looked into Murphy's gentle brown eyes and felt as if the dog understood what she was thinking.

Muffin, she thought, hesitant to share her news out loud. *I'm going to name her Muffin, a name that fits her more than Murphy.*

Paj spent the rest of the day and night with Murphy, petting her coat and feeding her from her hand. She tried to teach Murphy tricks but realized she already knew many. She sat on command, would stay, and come, wagging her tail as she relished the attention.

That night Murphy sat close to Paj, even though the younger cousins wanted to spend time with the furry new companion, too. Paj didn't mind when they whistled for Murphy to come to them.

The more people who became attached to Murphy, the less likely Mother and Father would say no to keeping her forever, Paj thought.

My plan might work after all, she hoped.

Murphy was friendly with the other children, but she knew who her main leader was and remained comfortable by Paj's side.

In such a short time, Paj already felt like she was Murphy's rightful new owner. She already felt so natural with Murphy, it was hard to believe she hadn't been loving this dog for years. Paj lay down on the ground next to Murphy and stroked her back, the fur shining gold in the fire's glow. Paj's arms cradled Murphy's neck. Closing her eyes to rest, allowing her weary body to finally relax, Murphy had said all she needed to.

Paj began to fall asleep, dozing and then startling awake to make sure Murphy was really there. The bright fire had lost its luster, dimming in the pitch black night. Paj's legs felt heavy from the hours they walked that day. Murphy seemed just as tired and just as happy to be right beside her new friend.

Paj stood to move to the tent she shared with her cousins and Murphy followed. At first Paj didn't think to bring Murphy inside, but Murphy stood so close, looking up expectantly when Paj went to unzip the tent; Paj struggled to stifle her laughter.

She decided to bring Murphy inside the tent to ensure she'd be there in the morning. Although Paj crept quietly so as not to wake the other children, Murphy didn't know to be as considerate. She stepped inside and someone in a dark sleeping sack pulled away. Paj couldn't help but laugh at her silly friend.

"Shhh….Here Muffin," she giggled.

They were settled in, but Paj had forgotten one thing. She had left food just outside the tent.

Chapter 19

Later that night Murphy barked, though she wasn't fully awake. Her keen sense of smell was like an alarm clock, alerting her to the fact that an intruder was near.

Something had clanged just outside the tent. Then a dull, slow crunching of branches could be heard underfoot.

Murphy growled softly and then barked again, this time waking Paj, who had been cozied next to Murphy as though they'd slept this way for years. The other children stirred in their sleep too. Although the air was cool outside, the heat of so much breath warmed them in their cocoon.

"Shhhh…." Paj said automatically, disoriented in her slumber. Then Paj heard movement outside the tent, just inches away. Only the thin side of the tent separated them from the unknown intruder. Wide awake, she lay frozen to her spot, gripping her blanket between tight fists.

The campfire long extinguished, there was no glow in order to see a shadow.

Paj knew that if she asked, "Who's there?" she wouldn't get a human reply.

She wanted Murphy to be still as well. She was worried that Murphy, alerting Paj to whatever was outside and seemed to want to come inside, was an obvious giveaway. Murphy continued to bark at the mysterious threat while Paj hoped that the clanging sound and movement would give way to silence. Something, or someone, paced back and forth in front of the tent; heavy footsteps were unconcerned, paying no heed to their lack of stealth.

Then, suddenly, everything was still. Murphy laid by Paj, easily sinking back into slumber despite Paj's rapid heartbeat. For Paj, sleep was not an option any longer. She was as awake then as if she had just run the mile at school.

A beam of light shined at the tent. "Everything okay?" Riam asked.

Paj couldn't answer; her whole body was tense. She swallowed and barely squeaked, "Yes."

The light went out and everything was quiet once more.

The next morning when Murphy and Paj exited the tent the metal bowl that held food for Murphy looked to have been tossed, 10 feet from where they had last seen it. There wasn't a trace of the squirrel stew that had been in it. It gleamed, it was so clean.

Paj picked up the bowl and went toward her mother, more concerned about her new friend's breakfast than her own.

Chu Cai gave Murphy a friendly pat as he walked past, but the others didn't pay as much attention to her as they had the day before. A pang of guilt shot through Paj when she remembered the dog collar, but she forced it away.

This is my dog now and her name is Muffin, Paj told herself. *She needs me, and I need her too.*

Chapter 20

Murphy was more energetic the second day and continued to eat as though she were making up for skipped meals which, unbeknownst to them, she was. Besides the occasional bird, Murphy had grown used to eating mostly bark and leaves in the wild, scavenging for whatever would fill her belly. Most of the time she made the right choice when she came upon brush, leaves, or berries she didn't recognize. However, there were also times when Murphy became violently ill after eating, emptying her insides of all the food she'd been able to gather, and more. Each time this happened, it depleted Murphy of any strength the food may have given her. By the time Paj found her, Murphy was in worse condition than she could have imagined.

Paj swallowed the lump in her throat and fought back the tears of sadness mixed with anger she felt just by thinking about leaving the mountains and going back to school. Sure, she'd had lots of different emotions on this trip, even fear, but she'd take any of them over shame. And that's what most of the kids at school made her feel.

Paj thought about the other students who called her weird or asked her embarrassing questions like, "Where does your Dad work?"

They knew the answer, but it was cruel of them to ask.

Responsibilities called Paj, but she wanted to stay in the mountains with Murphy, away from school and the mean kids, as long as possible. She wrestled with what she wanted to do and what she ought to do, until her good conscience won.

"Dad, I have school tomorrow," she said as her father walked past her, hoping he would be unfazed, but knowing it was the responsible thing to say.

"We need to hunt one more day," Riam replied as he wiggled his knit cap on his head. "And then we'll go back."

The fall hunting season was rapidly coming to an end. They raced against the first snow falling in the forest, the telltale signal that they had to pause until spring.

Upon hearing her father's words, Paj was glad she didn't have to choose. It was out of her control. Paj smiled at a funny thought. She couldn't go to school even if she had wanted to.

Chapter 21

The last morning at camp Riam and Chu Cai left at daybreak and stayed out all day. Paj was happy to stay with Murphy and felt more relaxed, even better rested, than she remembered feeling before Murphy came into her life.

As their camping trip was concluding, Paj didn't know what else she could do to sway her mother. Thinking about it consumed her. If nothing else, Paj decided on a strategy to ensure that Murphy wasn't a nuisance. If Murphy started to beg from one of the adults, Paj would quickly distract her or pull her away. If she was interacting with one of the children, Paj smiled, not so quick to step in. The more cousins who also fell in love with Murphy, the better.

"I thought Father would be back by now," Paj said as she counted soup bowls so Anh could ladle stew into them. They still had plenty more squirrels to take home and freeze for the winter.

"He hasn't gotten enough," Anh replied. "It will be too dark to pack up, so we will probably leave tomorrow."

Another day means another day they might change their minds about Muffin, Paj thought, still hoping she might have a chance to take Murphy home with them as she raced against the clock.

When the men returned at dusk, the full sack was slung over her uncle's shoulder this time.

"We tried to take her hunting but she wouldn't move," Chu Cai told Paj, pointing to Murphy. He described what had happened that morning at dawn as everyone at camp still slept. Chu Cai had peeked in the tent to see if Murphy would like to go hunting with them, but she stayed close to Paj's side, despite Chu Cai's tongue clucking and fingers snapping to come.

"She's lazy," Chu Cai laughed then, rolling up his sleeves as he walked over to get a bowl of hot stew.

Paj would have worried if she'd woken up to find Murphy gone, but she also wondered if Murphy had gone with her father and uncle, would it have guaranteed her a place in the family? Would they see how wonderful her new dog was, just as Paj had quickly learned?

As the sun lowered in the sky, casting a shadow across the campsite, Anh prepared another one of the squirrels from the earlier hunt, taking the time to fry it before adding it to the pot of bubbling carrots and potatoes in the large iron pot.

Murphy got up long enough to stand by the pot of boiling vegetables, sniffing the air. Then the hearty smell of squirrel meat rooted her to her spot.

Paj had expected to clean up after Murphy, to pick up dog poop, but she saw nothing the first day and then nothing the next. By the third day Paj still hadn't cleaned up any waste. Murphy still appeared to be very tired, just as she had been on the first day. She was content to lie next to the tent by her water bowl.

Then Paj smelled something putrid, like a dirty diaper left out in the baking sun. She got up and walked toward Murphy for a closer look and saw something brown smeared across her tail. Just a few feet away an explosion of diarrhea marked the border of their campsite. It was as though Murphy had tried to spare them from the accident, as though she wanted privacy, but couldn't quite make it to go away from their campsite.

As good as it tasted, she wasn't ready for it after eating next to nothing for so long. The large amount of rich foods had upset Murphy's stomach.

Paj looked around, trying to find a way to clean up the mess before anyone noticed when Anh came by with a broom, sweeping sticks and debris away to tidy up camp. She stopped to look at the mess. Her mouth turned down into a disgusted grimace and she turned away without a word.

Oh no, Paj thought. *Mother thinks Muffin is a*

nuisance.

Anh returned a minute later with a large bowl of water. She sloshed it on the mess. Most of it washed away, but a few chunks remained, stuck to the ground.

"You say goodbye to your new friend," Paj's mother said as soon as she finished. "We are leaving first thing in the morning."

"But I thought I could keep her!" Paj cried.

"No. She belongs here," Anh replied evenly.

Paj pleaded with her mother, but it was no use. Anh just kept going about her chores.

Once Father returned, he was not interested in Murphy coming home with them either.

"You found her here; she will stay here," he declared.

Paj swallowed, fighting back tears, deciding to tell them what she'd done with the collar in a last, desperate attempt to stay with her new friend.

"Muffin had an owner," she cried, finally getting both of her parents to look directly at her at once. "I threw away her collar, and now it's gone!"

Her voice broke and tears began to flow. "We can't just leave her here!"

Her parents continued to calmly look at her.

"If she can find us, she will find someone else," Riam said, softening his tone, concerned for his only child.

Despite his compassion, Riam's exhaustion was obvious; his face and voice remained firm. Tears or begging would not influence him. Paj knew her father well enough to know that.

Murphy stood by Paj's side, nudging her head under Paj's arm to be close. In that moment, Paj didn't think she could feel any sadder. Little did Murphy know, the two of them would be very far apart and the fact that Murphy had no clue was even more crushing to Paj.

If I had Muffin, Paj bartered in her mind, *I would go home and face anything at school, including bullies or embarrassment.*

She would gladly suffer any of those things if she could call Murphy her own, but Paj stopped short of telling her parents that.

Paj's parents had to tell her to hurry up, as she slowly gathered her things and rolled up her sleeping bag. They packed up their little camping home more quickly than usual. Just this once, Paj wished they would take their time. She never knew it was possible to feel pain for want of something so badly. When she hugged Murphy one last time and walked away to get in the pickup, she could barely breathe.

She felt the truck spring to life and then it hummed. Suddenly it rocked as Murphy was in the truck too—right next to Paj.

Wherever you go, so will I, Murphy's tail and eyes said. Paj sobbed, hugging Murphy close.

"I will never forget you," Paj cried, looking into Murphy's eyes and then rubbing her thumb between them. Murphy's tail beat with love for Paj.

She got out of the truck then and so did Murphy.

"Come on, let's go," Anh said. Paj got back in the truck and Anh reached over her to slam the door closed, leaving Murphy standing alone in the empty campsite.

Chu Cai and his family were already starting to move. The little truck packed with Paj's family and all their supplies soon followed.

Paj glanced back at Murphy, who was panting as she looked toward Paj.

Wait a minute, Murphy's wagging tail asked. *Where are you going?*

As the vehicles crept down the long dirt road, leading out of the campsite, Paj stared out the back window at Murphy standing all alone. Murphy turned away just then to look for an opening in a trash bag one of the adults had left secured. She was intent, sniffing it, pacing around it, serious about finding her next meal.

"Good luck, Muffin," Paj said softly. As she and her family turned a corner, Murphy disappeared from sight and immediately the hectic pace of life and all of the complexities Paj knew she'd face once back at home, enveloped her.

Chapter 22

A good night's sleep was rare for Nathan and Erin once Murphy went missing. For one thing, they couldn't get comfortable because Murphy had always slept not just at the foot of their bed, but right in between them. Now when they went to sleep, the void created by Murphy's disappearance wasn't just in their hearts; they could literally feel it.

Where is Murphy sleeping now? They wondered all day, every day.

Maybe someone else is taking care of Murphy, loving her, Erin thought when she chose to think positively. The image of another person taking care of Murphy made her feel better. Someone else was playing fetch with her. Someone else was kissing her between the eyes. Some other family was looking at her with the same love in their eyes that the Brauns had. That image brought Erin peace.

On the very first day of searching for Murphy, Erin and Nathan's extended family and friends canvassed every part of the region where Nathan had last seen her. They reconvened each night, either in person or by text, to tell their tales of the day.

Erin's sister, Mary, and her husband, Mike, were the first ones to head up to Hell Hole to search. Mike had a bad foot from a motorcycle injury that happened years before. Although he wasn't much of a hiker, he was a great dirt bike rider. He took the day off work, packed his dirt bike, and scoured the mountains to search for Murphy. A self-proclaimed "dog whisperer," Mike knew if anyone could lure a scared pup back to safety it was him. While Mary hiked on foot, Mike took the bike miles into the terrain, a dog harness close at hand in case he found Murphy. He kept expecting to see Murphy when he'd come around each blind turn. Nothing was ever there to greet him except the occasional squirrel, which would look him square in the eye before quickly scampering for cover.

Their good friends and neighbors, Jason and Lauren Anderson, headed up to Hell Hole to help with the search too. They brought their dog, Samson, who they had always jokingly referred to as Murphy's boyfriend. This time the story couldn't have been more true, as Samson bravely combed the forest with his parents, natural athletes with hearts of gold, to find their friend.

They'd stumbled upon a black bear while driving

through the winding roads, but they weren't deterred. Once on foot, any concern they had about encountering the bear without being in the safety of their truck was eclipsed by their perseverance to find Murphy.

Within 24 hours Erin reached out to Homeward Bound Golden Retriever Rescue, with the hope that the organization's larger community of volunteers would be able to help find Murphy. The Homeward Bound team of volunteers were like angels to Nathan and Erin. They provided a lifeline as they immediately sent word to their network in the surrounding regions of Foresthill, Georgetown, and up to the Tahoe Basin communities.

Many hands, eyes, and ears aided them in their search. Having so much help was the only thing that eased the nagging feeling that they should be doing more. The Rescue encouraged them to set up a Facebook page about Murphy, which was shared many times and served as the command post. The news about Murphy being lost spread fast, and soon people from all over Northern California were spending their weekends helping to search for her. To the Brauns, the Rescue was a godsend.

It was reassuring that so many others aided in the search. When the Brauns began to see posters of Murphy that they hadn't posted, they realized that they were not on their journey alone. So many people who had never even met Murphy cared about her. The outpouring of support the Brauns received

This dog was named after Earl Louis "Curly" Lambeau, the former Green Bay Packers coach.

When Murphy was lost, it was Lambeau's joy that disappeared. She had to be encouraged to eat and she only wanted to sleep where Murphy's scent was strongest.

With Murphy's absence, things were not the same for any of the Brauns, even for the youngest member of the family, baby Finegan.

Finegan has never known a time before Murphy, Erin often thought as time passed.

Like everyone else Finegan loved Murphy from the start, but Murphy seemed anxious when Finegan was first born. She wasn't sure of this tiny object, swaddled in a blanket, that everyone gathered around. Erin had been gone and then returned with this little thing who didn't do much from Murphy's vantage point. When Murphy tried jumping up into bed with Nathan and Erin, she was shooed away. The little blanket that everyone looked at was between her parents in the bed, instead. Lullaby voices and sweet caresses weren't saved for her, but for this little blanket.

Murphy would pace back and forth and nudge under Erin's arm with her nose for a pat.

I'm here too, Murphy pleaded with her eyes.

Yet those days were fleeting. As soon as the little blanket transitioned into a little person who smiled and reached for Murphy, she grew protective of the little guy, and enjoyed the bonus high chair scraps.

The first few weeks that Murphy went missing Finegan, only a year old, toddled to Murphy's pet bed in the family room and laid down in it.

"Murph!" he'd call.

Seeing Finegan and Murphy snuggling in that bed used to make Erin's heart glad, but the image of Finegan all alone in that bed accentuated the negative space created by Murphy's absence.

Then, after a few weeks, Finegan stopped asking and didn't remember to say "Murph" any longer.

The Brauns wanted to keep smiling, so they retold the funny stories of Murphy as a puppy. She had always been a chewer. She chewed on socks, the corners of blankets, and the kitchen table.

She peed on everything, too, and jumped the fence to take a swim in the pool whenever she felt like it.

Instead, Erin stared outside at the placid, vacant water. She longed for one of those earlier, frustrating times when she was annoyed with Murphy. One look into those big, brown eyes that always expressed, "I love you so much!" and Erin could never stay mad for long.

Those memories made Erin smile and gave her hope whenever she worried about Murphy's whereabouts.

Where is she sleeping? Is she hungry? Is she cold? Erin wondered.

Erin must have asked a hundred times if Murphy had her collar on when they last saw her, and Nathan always assured her that she did.

But if someone did have her, why wouldn't the person call? Erin thought.

And then there was the question Erin asked on days when she didn't think they could search anymore, when the miles were racking up on the car, and when their feet were sore from searching on foot. She tossed and turned at night with one thought, the last thought she'd have before finally surrendering to sleep—*Was Murphy alive?*

Chapter 23

For the first few months, the phone often rang with news of possible sightings. Each time Erin or Nathan could be heard saying, "Oh really?" it was clear what that meant and what they'd do next. Undoubtedly they'd be energized to make the trip back to the mountains.

They scoured the region from South Lake Tahoe to North Lake Tahoe, and the miles upon miles of forest in between, but the sightings always turned out to be a different dog. It was not a golden retriever, but another breed most of the time. They would rush back to the mountains to where a dog was being held for them only to be greeted by a lab, an Akita, a German shepherd or, when their hearts drummed because they saw a golden retriever that looked like Murphy, they'd take a closer look only to find it wasn't her. Once they raced to South Lake Tahoe only to learn that the cute dog at the golden retriever rescue wasn't Murphy, but a male dog who also needed to get back to his home.

Even more friends, family members, and strangers arrived to help search. It was the only thing that brought the Brauns comfort and gave them strength—to know that so many people were helping them. They were not alone.

While Nathan searched the mountains and forest, Erin generally commanded the search from home. With the help of friends, family, and strangers who were fast becoming friends, they still wondered if they could do more.

Nathan spent $2,500 to take a search dog to the place where that fateful camping trip first began at Worton's Market in Foresthill, but because of rain and countless other visitors, the dog couldn't find Murphy's scent.

Three weeks after they last saw Murphy, the phone rang at the house. The caller described a sure sighting of Murphy and even mentioned the found dog seemed scared and lost, before she had taken off again. The caller also described seeing the mystery dog wearing a brown collar. Erin called her brother-in-law and within minutes they jumped in his truck with his son and sped up the hill to South Lake Tahoe.

"We need to get there before it gets dark," Erin told him. The truck was lightning fast, cutting the usual 90-minute drive in half, arriving at dusk. As soon as they got to the hot spot, where a dog who looked just like Murphy was last seen, her brother-in-law drove slowly while Erin and her nephew got out on foot, whistling for the dog that eluded them. Remembering her brother-in-law's magnetic gift with dogs, Erin thought, *Mike will find Murphy and coax her into the car…Let's just have this be over.*

Nothing.

They raised their voices, then screamed, "Murphy!" until their throats hurt.

Still nothing.

Once it was dark it became clear that they would be going home without Murphy yet again, but they decided to target South Lake Tahoe as a spot to leave more fliers.

That weekend their army of volunteers set up a base camp at a coffee shop and volunteers from Homeward Bound helped look for her.

Every weekend for the next eight weeks, would be the same.

Chapter 24

Nathan had just strapped Finegan into a baby carrier backpack he wore before beginning another day of posting more lost dog posters, while friends and even strangers were out doing the same. Together they had already left their mark, or Murphy's mark, across two counties. They focused on the foothills and just beyond where Murphy went missing, in the more populated Lake Tahoe region.

As Nathan secured what seemed like the millionth paper with the identical picture of Murphy on the front of a tree, a man driving by noticed him. What really got his attention, and made him decide to pull over, was seeing a baby on Nathan's back.

The man got out of his car and walked directly to Nathan and Finegan. He scanned the sign that was now attached to the tree, but didn't have to read much beyond MISSING to know what to do next.

"I'd like to help," the man called out, leaving his

car parked on the side of the road. He was dressed in slacks and a long-sleeved dress shirt as though he were on his way to work.

Nathan was surprised and couldn't help but grin, humbled by yet another stranger's support. He was reminded that there are far more good people in the world, people who want to help others, than there are bad ones.

"Thank you," Nathan said, reaching to shake the man's hand. "I'll bet you didn't think you'd be posting signs when you woke up this morning."

"If you can be out here doing that with your baby on your back, well, I'd like to help too," the man clarified, beginning to roll up his sleeves.

Nathan smiled, handing him a stack of white posters before talking strategy. They decided that the man would post them on the route he was taking to the office, an area that as far as Nathan knew hadn't yet been covered.

In the first three months of the search, concentrating on his job was difficult because Nathan spent all of his free time looking for Murphy. And when he was at work, he was still thinking about Murphy. He and Erin jumped every time the phone rang, ready to drive back up the mountain as they had so many times before.

Rings of exhaustion began to form under Nathan's eyes as he hadn't felt truly relaxed, nor had he gotten a restful night sleep, since the day they last saw Murphy. As much as his body wanted to shut off and not think about every possibility as well as the should-haves, would-haves, or could-haves, it was as though Nathan's brain stood with a yardstick, rapping his body with it if he dared to take a break.

The Brauns dreamed to hear the words, "Murphy is doing fine and coming home…This was all just a terrible misunderstanding." But as each day, each week, and then each month passed, the nightmare wouldn't end.

Over the months those hope-filled words, "We may have found your dog," were heard less and less, so Nathan's pulse beat like a drum once he absorbed what he heard from one caller, and especially that the caller was so persistent. The caller described a sighting he encountered every morning in South Lake Tahoe, in an open space by a motel. At first they had been skeptical of the caller, a grocery store clerk who had seen the lost dog signs. He hadn't called just once, but four days in a row to say that a golden retriever was hanging around the grocery store's trash area and that the dog would come back at the same time every day, before retreating back to the open space.

The Brauns thought this sighting seemed different, so they decided to drive the two hours to Lake Tahoe. They checked into the motel just long enough to drop their bags so that they could start searching as soon as possible.

They decided to start at the open space, where the caller said the dog would retreat after scouring for food at the grocery store.

Once they got close to the field, the sense of Murphy was strong. Erin didn't waste a second, rolling down the window to yell, "Murphy!"

I remember all of the times Murphy ran to greet us at the door, Erin thought, as she still expected Murphy to come bounding toward her at any moment. *If she could hear me she would come…Where could she possibly be?*

They searched the meadow, the wide expanse of grass that had turned brown in the bitterness of winter, splotched with intermittent patches of snow.

They looked back and forth, as far as their eyes could see. There could be no hiding in this clearing. The only sound they heard was the whisper of the wind. Then an owl hooted, ready to go back to sleep for the day.

"Let's go back to the shopping center," Erin said.

They backtracked across the street to their car and, like a top secret stakeout, waited for 90 minutes in the parking lot, looking for clues. Someone didn't find it as exciting, however. Finegan started to whine in the backseat, letting them know he'd had enough. Just as Erin and Nathan's thoughts began to wander and their alertness began to give way to fatigue, Erin turned her head to look back at Finegan when something caught her attention. Erin's gaze zeroed in on a golden dog just out the window. With ribs visible, the animal was sniffing the garbage dumpsters, looking for something, anything to eat, seemingly without another care in the world.

To the Brauns a more beautiful sight could not

have been imagined, by a garbage dumpster no less.

"Do you see that?" Nathan stammered, without taking his eyes off the mystery dog.

Before Erin had a chance to say she did, they were opening the doors of the truck, rushing but also trying to be covert so as not to startle the unsuspecting animal. Nathan slammed the door in excitement and the dog stopped to look at them. Nathan tiptoed in its direction as Erin reached in to deftly unbuckle Finegan. Together the three of them trod lightly, trying not to alarm him or her, shielding their excitement with all their will. The dog turned back to look for food, unimpressed with their presence.

Just as the Brauns were within arms' reach, the dog took off, fleeing for the wide, open space across the street. With Finegan resting on Erin's hip, she and Nathan set off to catch a closer look at the Murphy doppelganger on foot. With hearts pounding, husband and wife both thought, *This is it.*

"Murphy," Nathan called in a friendly voice, but the dog trotted ahead, not showing any sign of recognition at the sound of the name.

Nathan held up a piece of bacon. "Come here girl," he called, dangling the tempting morsel in the air. He'd grown accustomed to bringing such lures with him on searches.

The dog stopped and turned, nose sniffing the air as it began to walk toward them.

"That's a girl," Erin said, her heart hammering in

her chest.

When the dog was close enough for them to touch, Nathan tilted his head sideways and said, "It's a boy." Nathan patted the approaching dog and offered a piece of the bacon bait. The dog snatched it, wolfing it down in one gulp before proceeding to turn and run away, leaving the Brauns stunned from the letdown.

In the coming weeks, and then months, as they continued to comb Lake Tahoe and its surrounding towns, the searches blended together, becoming one continuous blur. They would search all day, every weekend, supplying coffee and donuts for volunteers as thanks for their efforts and with the hopes that they'd keep coming back with more searchers in tow. At the end of each weekend they hadn't found Murphy, but Erin and Nathan made many new friends and learned more than they ever thought they would about the region. They'd come to know every gas station, every motel, every hotel, and every restaurant in the area as they continued to post lost dog fliers and inquire if anyone had seen their missing golden retriever.

One man they met through the animal rescue earned the nickname "The Voice of Reason" because animals gravitated toward him. If they could just spot Murphy, surely she would come to him too. "If I spot Murphy, she'll come to me. I guarantee it," he would say. Once, this man who only months before had been a stranger, rode his bike from Truckee to South

Shore, crossing the entirety of Lake Tahoe, just to look for Murphy.

As much as Nathan wanted to stay close to home so he could jump in the car and drive up to the mountains whenever there was a new lead, he had to get back to traveling for work.

His first business trip was tough. When he got off the plane in Colorado Springs he went for a walk to clear his mind. He happened to walk right past a church. He'd grown accustomed to operating on auto pilot, his single focus on looking for Murphy while still keeping his family and job together. He'd started to drown out periphery distractions. So it was a surprise, even to Nathan, that he felt pulled to go inside the unfamiliar church. But once he made the choice to turn and go in, Nathan instantly felt peace wash over him.

The same thing occurred a few weeks later while Nathan searched in South Lake Tahoe for what felt like the millionth time. As he approached an intersection shaped like a Y, an intersection he'd taken many times before, Nathan saw it with new eyes and suddenly wasn't sure which way to turn. It was early winter by then, cold and damp. As Nathan pondered which way to go he saw a sign leading to the right that read, "Say a prayer, get a cup of coffee."

Nathan decided that was the perfect thing to do.

Chapter 25

The welcoming mood, and the easy meals, left when Paj and her family did. Murphy would have to forage for food once more. She knocked over garbage bins at campsites whenever she could, but no matter what she ate, she was always ravenous.

The persistent ache in Murphy's belly kept her awake. She faced a dilemma. It was easier to stay hidden in the forest, but with the solitude it was also harder to find food. She had to keep moving and she had one purpose in life: to eat.

A treasured find was a littered, empty cookie bag that contained a few crumbs. They were delicious crumbs, but as everything Murphy found these days, there were too few. Murphy pushed her nose into one tattered sack, desperate for any speck she could get. She smelled something different in the air and followed the scent to the water faucet, where campers clean pans or fill them with water. Gooey pancake batter congealed at the bottom of the faucet. Each drop of water, coupled with the sticky batter beneath it, expanded the gooey substance, making it that day's most substantial meal. Murphy licked, turning her head at impossible angles to get every last bit, picking up more dirt than batter, but it was worth it. She'd gladly eat a bucket of dirt for even a tablespoon of the delicious goo. The sugar spread through her body, making her feel warm. But like everything she ate on her own in the forest, Murphy could never get enough and it was always gone too soon.

Dirt, leaves, and twigs stuck to Murphy because of sticky syrup stuck to her fur from an earlier food reconnaissance. Murphy had rummaged a paper plate out of a plastic bag that still had perfectly good pancakes and little chunks of sausage clinging to it. It had been late enough in the day that whomever the garbage had belonged to was away from camp, probably hiking or swimming in the river. Murphy had to tear a hole in the garbage bag, ripping it wider with each discovery she saw inside, including three paper plates covered with pizza sauce and plastered cheese, which she demolished, plates and all.

A violent rumble filled Murphy's stomach and she threw up much of what she'd just eaten. She licked a little at the vomit and felt better.

Murphy sniffed the ground around a picnic table. She smelled something on the bar at the base of it, something that had spilled, and licked it. Just then, a growl interrupted her investigation.

Murphy turned to see an animal staring at her, yet the flash in its eyes was not friendly; it saw lunch. A wolverine looking for meat, the weasel-like creature came closer. Teeth gnashing, it wanted to fight; or did it want to eat?

Murphy was frightened by the look in the wolverine's eyes but her body didn't have the energy to fight. She turned and fled into the woods, away from the campsite. It certainly wasn't safer in the shrouded forest, but Murphy sensed anywhere was better than staying near something that wanted to harm her.

Chapter 26

Murphy was startled awake. The crunch, crunching of heavy footsteps approaching perked up her ears and in an instant she was standing. Murphy's instinct was to run from the sound, a stark difference from her nature before. When she was in the comfort of her home with the Brauns, she would run straight to unknown sounds, but no longer. Fear and suspicion had crowded out her former curious and trusting self. Murphy turned in the other direction, running from the footsteps before she could see to whom they belonged.

A search volunteer stopped and looked in the direction Murphy had gone. Had he known the rustlings he heard through the forest were Murphy, and not a wild animal, he would have given chase. Little did he know that Murphy was already becoming a wild animal.

The volunteer looked in the direction of the scattering of twigs and dried leaves, and though he couldn't see anything, his sense was that some other living thing was near. "Murphy?" he called. The blowing of the early winter wind was the only response. A stack of lost dog posters in his hand, the volunteer peered, trying to see beyond the cluster of trees that barricaded what secrets lay behind them.

Murphy struggled up a slight hill, her blood pumping, wanting nothing but seclusion. She stopped and cocked her head when she heard a familiar word, "Murphy," but then kept moving.

Chapter 27

With the first snow fall, fewer sighting calls came in. When the phone did ring, Erin and Nathan were more careful, guarding themselves from disappointment. So many false leads that didn't turn out to be Murphy became too much to bear. While they used to jump at every sighting that sounded plausible, now they began to ask more questions, to be more circumspect, before driving back to the mountains. Instead of allowing themselves to feel frenzied, they trained their minds to remain calm.

Their consistent group of search volunteers dropped right along with the freezing temperatures.

The frigid days and even colder nights also brought the realization that Murphy may not have survived. Yet the one, remaining flicker of hope that there was a slight chance Murphy could still be alive fueled them more than thinking about the 98 percent chance that she was not.

Staying positive and channeling their energy into finding Murphy also made the Brauns feel less anxious. Nathan and Matthew went camping every chance they could. When the sounds of countless voices calling her name didn't bring her out of hiding, the Brauns were certain that familiar smells would do it. Nathan and Matthew cooked bacon whenever they could, at home before they set off on a search, and it was also the first thing they did at their campsites, even before they'd pitched their tent. Then they would wait, hoping to lead Murphy back to them via a scent trail, just as the large, floating cloud in cartoons makes everyone a follower.

Just before Christmas, Matthew and Morgan made their wish list for Santa, as they always did. They worked intently, deep into their writing, stopping only to whisper a bit to each other. Once they were finished with their work they looked at their parents and smiled, sliding their lists across the kitchen countertop. They'd even made a list for Finegan.

Erin and Nathan smiled as they reached for the pieces of paper, but as they read and then looked at each other, locking eyes, their smiles faded.

Finegan's list read:

> *Fuzzy Elmo jacket*
> *Bring Murphy home safe*
> *Cool monster toy*

Elmo movies

Morgan's list read:

Dork Diary books
Murphy to come back home safe

Matthew's list read:

Bring our Murphy home safe
Electric scooter

It broke Erin's and Nathan's hearts that the kids each asked for the one thing money couldn't buy. How would Santa be able to bring them this gift?

"I'm not sure even Santa can get you this present, to bring Murphy back," Erin gently told the children.

Determination fiery in her eyes, Morgan responded, "But Santa's magic. He can do anything."

Chapter 28

Just after Christmas, 2012 Nathan posted an update on the Murphy Braun Facebook page.

Friends, it is with a heavy heart and many mixed emotions that I must write this message to you. My family and I have decided to put a reunion with Murphy in the hands of God. We have done all we can to bring her home safely including hiring a dog tracker, posting/handing out numerous fliers and advertisements on social and print media, hours of searching by foot and car, and most of all, utilizing the help from the great community of dog lovers throughout the Lake Tahoe basin, Georgetown/Foresthill and other parts of California who have dedicated numerous hours to the search efforts.

I spent Sunday (December 9, 2012) on a hike with Lambeau (our one-year-old golden retriever) and hiked back into the camping spot at Hell Hole Reservoir. She and I searched and called for Murphy the entire eight miles, with no results. While most people believe she has made her way out of the canyon, I find peace in our family's decision to cease all physical search efforts.

We have been blessed with Murphy's presence for the past five years and while we are not giving up hope, we find it necessary to give up the search. Again, we can't begin to thank the numerous volunteers who have dedicated their time, efforts, and resources to contribute to the search. We have had numerous calls and presumed sightings that have never materialized in Murphy's return but have aided in the reunion of other lost pets with their owners. Through this process we have been exposed to a different level of humanity often not found in society today. People who have never met Murphy or my family have opened their hearts to help find our beloved dog and have gone through great lengths to help.

While some people may disagree with our decision to pull back on the search, I ask that you will adhere to our decision. Erin and I need to continue to be strong for our three children—which their number one request this holiday season was to bring Murphy home safely. As we move forward, we will still be involved with certain elements of social and print media and hope our prayers will someday be answered and that someone will call when they have her in their arms. We will still provide a reward for her safe return.

Thank you again for the generous gifts of your time, dedication, and hope in bringing Murphy home.

The Braun Family

Chapter 29

Like when Sleeping Beauty and her village slumbered while under a spell, the forest, too, paused that winter. While many animals slept like statues during their annual hibernation, each day the forest grew increasingly quiet.

Regardless of the light snow and the chilly air, some animals remained alert. The high-pitched calls of the pika remained constant each day, fading at dusk. The small rodents look like a cross between a rabbit and a guinea pig. Their distinct calls end just as the rustling of nocturnal animals begin. These were the animals who were left, those who didn't store up and eat a bounty in the spring and summer. These animals were hungry all the time.

Once the sun nestled below the horizon it was

then that owls, skunks, and raccoons made themselves known in the darkness, taking charge as leaders of the night patrol.

Murphy learned the hard way how skunks protect themselves. She'd never seen anything like them, those critters with the large white stripe shocked down their black bodies. One night she had the misfortune to encounter one.

Murphy trailed a skunk through a clearing in the woods. For the first time in a while, Murphy felt playful and desired the harmless looking animal's attention. The flashes of being carefree came and went. More often than not Murphy was on defense, quick to flit away, surprising even herself in the rare instances when she attacked.

The skunk picked up its pace, darting this way and that as Murphy chased it. Her fear and loneliness were forgotten. In her mind, Murphy was back in her yard, chasing a squirrel.

Just as Murphy was about to reach the skunk it stopped, raised its tail, and sped on. Murphy was left standing in its noxious mist. She was immobile, overtaken by a horrid stench that paralyzed her body with its strength. Only her eyes showed signs of life, welling with tears. Through blurred vision, Murphy watched the skunk scurry across the light dusting of snow on the forest floor before disappearing from sight.

Murphy would continue to see at least one skunk every night after that, but as soon as she saw that white stripe, Murphy knew to go in the other direction.

As the snow continued to fall, the forest grew still. The potential for hunting meat all but disappeared, just as the steady flow of leaves and twigs, a staple of Murphy's diet, did too. Murphy hunted for anything she could eat, but above all else she yearned for meat. A fallen bird or a distracted chipmunk would do, and she was lucky to get either.

At the end of one long day, sniffing in the forest for any sign of life, Murphy was surprised when she encountered another animal that made her instantly cower, her defenses raised in alert.

The sun was setting and Murphy had stopped to rest near a tree, when she felt eyes upon her. Another dog looked intently her way, its steely eyes locking with hers. Murphy got up to walk closer, but the coyote stood transfixed to its spot. With tannish, gray fur and perked up ears, the coyote was smaller than Murphy, but a lifetime of living in the wild had made her a skilled hunter. During the winter it was a matter of survival that the coyote be more active in the daylight to find food. Compared to Murphy, who had grown weary and slow, the coyote was practically frisky.

She continued to look at Murphy from a short distance away, licking her lips. The coyote broke the stare first, turning her head down to continue working at something more intriguing to her, a single tree blocking whatever it was from Murphy's view.

The coyote's serious eyes shot back to Murphy's as if to dare, *Join me.* She looked away slowly, turning back to her important work, beginning to pull it, then struggling to drag the weight of whatever it was.

Interested, Murphy cautiously walked closer to the action and watched as the coyote lowered her head and pecked slowly. Murphy walked closer still for a better look, sensing danger, but the hunger pangs in her stomach overrode whatever fear she had. The smell, even from a distance, was intoxicating. She feasted on a small deer.

Four coyote pups appeared from the brush to join their mother. They were like children running in from playing outside, gathering around the family dinner table to share a meal. Murphy stopped to survey the scene.

Despite their smaller size, the pups looked just like their mother. All of them had the same golden, mysterious eyes and deep hunger for meat.

Murphy edged closer to the pack as the coyotes continued to devour the deer, their coveted treat, not seeming to notice, or care, that she was there. Murphy inched even closer, sniffing the air. She smelled the fresh meat that the wild dogs enjoyed, getting some satisfaction from its scent alone. Yet the satisfaction was fickle. Within seconds the smell tormented her, tugging at her insides, making her mouth turn dry and pasty, tricked by its inability to form saliva as dehydration set in.

Murphy was close enough to the pack to touch

any one of the wild dogs, but they still didn't seem to mind she was there, though her instinct told her otherwise. She got close enough to the pack to reach down and lick the deer; a test. Would they show her she wasn't welcome? Would they attack? She scampered back as though dodging an invisible blow, but the group just kept on eating as if she were not there.

Murphy walked carefully back to the pack. She looked down at the deer, the chunks of bloody pink flesh disappearing with each bite. How she longed for one taste.

As her sights were set on the delicious extravagance, she glanced back at the coyotes again to make sure she was welcome, to make sure she was safe, but the coyotes paid her no mind and continued to feast.

Murphy took one quick, energizing bite and then, when nothing happened, she ate more. As each bite gave her a shot of confidence and the needed nourishment to last another day, it was too late to stop.

Just as she relaxed, focused on the all-important task at hand, a searing jolt grabbed Murphy's hind leg. The mother had nipped her, sending the unwelcoming message, "Get away!"

Murphy yelped in pain and ran from the scene.

Mother coyote turned back to her meal, the nuisance of Murphy forgotten. She joined the others as Murphy watched from a distance, sticky spittle pasty in her dry mouth, as the coyotes cleaned out the deer.

Once Mother coolly turned to go, the rest followed.

Chapter 30

The next morning Murphy woke from her outdoor bed beneath a tree to see a coyote pup trotting back and forth just a few feet away from her, looking to play. The mother coyote and the rest of the pups had returned to finish their deer leftovers. Murphy watched as they ate the last pink remnants of its carcass, leaving only one trace it had ever existed—its pelt. As much as she wanted to join in, Murphy stayed away. When the playful pup came even closer to Murphy, she stood and sniffed the baby.

The mother glanced her way and Murphy stopped, readying to escape should the wild dog attack. Instead, the mother turned to go and, just as the night before, the others followed. She looked back at Murphy as if to say, "Come along if you wish."

Murphy didn't hesitate, following with eyes downcast, careful not to get too close. It was more than a desire to follow the leader, or even to play. Murphy followed as a matter of survival, something instinctive that she knew would keep her alive, would help her find food in the quiet, barren forest.

Murphy would remain with the pack of coyotes that winter. There were times she felt threatened, never fully at home with this new family. When she sensed danger Murphy cautiously kept her distance, a harmless straggler who remained for the moments she could get what was most important to them all: food. Although sustenance was harder to find in the winter, with the pack Murphy still ate much better than she would have on her own. Just as the saying goes, "Better the devil you know than the devil you don't," Murphy found the closest thing to safety was to remain with the coyote pack. Deep down Murphy knew this would allow her to fare better than being alone.

As long as Murphy was tolerated by the coyotes, she would continue to get food. She learned quickly to keep her eyes down and never make the pack feel threatened. If they felt alarmed by her presence it would surely mean isolation, or worse, starvation. Murphy helped with the younger pups whenever she could.

Once, when one of the pups played a few feet away from the group, Murphy saw a gray wolf leering at it from a distance. As quick as a mother's instincts,

Murphy lunged for the pup and carried it in her mouth back within the vicinity of its mother's safe gaze.

The wolf was left to lick its lips, only imagining what a fine lunch the young, tender pup would make, and hid behind some brush. She settled into her new role. While the pups played Murphy remained alert, the perfect babysitter.

She learned a new skill she never knew in her former domestic life, which was gauged only by loneliness, play, love, and hunger. Murphy learned it was smart to stay in the background and only make herself known when she was needed. She didn't try to take a leadership role, but stood in line and waited to see what was left for her. When the mother coyote killed a larger animal like a mule deer, Murphy took her cue when it was time to get her share. When one of the coyotes killed a small rodent, Murphy waited for any offering, but didn't expect one. Her inclination to act quickly had turned into a subdued resolve that with patience, she would get more.

When one coyote howled, and then another, Murphy joined in the chorus but was never the one to start it. She was grateful for the pack's companionship, which meant everything to her.

By then, Murphy's prime motivator had changed from play and friendship to something more important—maintaining obscurity to ensure a good meal.

Chapter 31

When Erin felt sad, or allowed herself to think the worst, she had a recurring dream. Multiple sets of glowing eyes, the cartoon kind, lit up the darkness. Disembodied voices snarled and sneered, licking their lips, as the eyes moved closer to their catch to gobble it up. At this point in Erin's dream Murphy always appeared and a spotlight fell squarely on her, while the blood thirsty creatures remained caped in darkness. All alone, Murphy would back up, bumping into one of the beasts hidden behind her.

In this dream, their mangy bodies thrust into sight as the moon illuminated their bared fangs. Murphy was surrounded. As they pounced on Murphy all at once, it was then Erin could tell that the animals were coyotes.

In this nightmare Erin always felt the same way.

She was restless in her sleep as she wished for Murphy's struggle to be over. She pleaded for the ripping and the gnashing of teeth, for Murphy's yips and yelps, to give way to calm and surrender.

Erin would always wake from the same nightmare she'd have countless times to think, *I hope it was quick.*

One morning, after such a dream, one of Erin's co-workers asked if she thought Murphy was still alive. Whenever anyone asked, Erin's response was always a hopeful, "Yes."

When she looked into the co-worker's eyes Erin saw the same, sympathetic look she and Nathan had grown used to from other people.

"I really think she is," Erin expanded, not letting doubt creep into her voice. She always answered in the positive when people asked, not only because she wanted to believe it, but it gave her hope, and the hope gave her strength. Then there was another feeling, something she couldn't describe, that told her Murphy was still hanging on out there.

The co-worker's eyes said what she was really thinking. She may as well have said, "You're so naïve. Can't you see the obvious?"

"How do you think she's surviving?" the woman asked, walking but twisting her torso to look straight at Erin, searching to see if there was something Erin might not want to show.

The question hadn't come as a surprise. In fact, *How do you think she is surviving?* was the same, repetitive question Erin asked herself every day. It was the thought that kept her awake at night. It was always her last thought before she went to sleep.

Sure, she believed Murphy was still alive; she knew it, but still she cringed to think what she must be enduring out there all alone.

On good days Erin hoped someone had taken Murphy to a new home. Even if that meant they'd never see her again, at least it meant Murphy was alive and hopefully happy with a roof over her head.

Before dinner that night their neighbor, Randy, stopped by to drop off mail that was accidentally delivered to him.

Randy stood on the porch. After exchanging pleasantries, he asked, "Any news?"

Nathan and Erin had grown used to these almost daily conversations with others about Murphy. Besides the sympathetic eyes these conversations often triggered, other people almost always began sharing their own lost pet stories or even miracle stories they had heard before. There had been a dog who vanished after a tornado in Alabama. That family had been sure their pet had died; three weeks later the dog appeared on its owner's doorsteps with two broken legs.

There was also a five-week-old kitten from Arizona that was discovered in California after surviving a 400-mile road trip inside a car bumper.

There were plenty of miracle stories. The Brauns didn't lose hope that Murphy could be one of them.

Randy was the neighbor who liked to offer his

experience in order to relate to the situation. He was very sympathetic to Murphy's disappearance and had even grown to love her, yet he was always one who could help others understand that in life things happen for a reason. He gave up both sides of the argument of whether she was alive or gone, and always had an intellectual reason as to what could have happened to her. He was glad to hear that the Brauns had hadn't given up hope because miracles do happen; believe it or not.

Once, in an awkward encounter, an acquaintance shared a story when he wasn't sure what to say, "We had an old cat who wandered off from our cabin once."

He recalled how his teenage son, who was only eight at the time, found their cat not far from the cabin two days later, except something else had found the cat first.

"Flies were swarming his body," the man said as Erin grimaced Then he looked off into the distance before adding, "Toby never got that image of Pepper out of his mind."

Erin nodded politely. She looked over to be sure the kids couldn't hear.

"Toby's 17 now but whenever Pepper comes up, he always talks about how he looked that day."

He paused, then lowered his voice. "We remind him of good stuff, like how he was surprised to get Pepper as a little kitten on Christmas." Then, perking up, "I'll never forget how happy he was, and the surprise was something I'll never forget."

Erin smiled.

"But no," the man sighed. "Whenever Pepper comes up, Toby just says how he saw all those flies buzzing around and how Pepper looked so different."

Erin nodded patiently, remembering that people were just trying to help. While grateful that this person who she had never said more than a sentence to before was trying to make a connection, Erin still couldn't help but think, *Sometimes people say the strangest things.*

"And this other time, when Toby was a baby, we were sure we lost a cat," he continued while Erin just wanted the conversation to end. She had been in a much better mood before she'd encountered him.

"It was just gone one day, boom, just like that," he said, his pace picking up with the action. "Then about a year later the craziest thing happened. Like a ghost, that cat turned up, living just around the corner with a neighbor we didn't know. She even came when we called her and she meowed like crazy, but, get this, she had a name tag on with another name on it!"

"Wow," Erin replied, this time actually feeling a little better, more hopeful, about Murphy's fate.

"We kind of laughed it was so weird, but decided to leave well enough alone," he added, hands relaxed in his pockets. "We figured the cat had been through enough confusion."

Chapter 32

Spring 2013

As the snow began to melt, the American River swelled. The mother coyote had just given birth to a new litter, four pups this time, and their older siblings had already left the pack to go out on their own.

The pack had several dens in the area, moving from one to another for safety. They recently found an easy meal when they returned to a modest home by the river to find a family of mice taking up residence. After the coyotes barged in and broke up the family gathering by eating the mouse family, they moved in.

The early spring sunshine felt good. The coyotes basked in it, relaxing close to the muddy edges by the river. Mother licked her lips and in turn washed each of her cubs, just as mothers around the world ready their children for school. The pups relished her attention, returning her affection by attempting to lick their mother with their little pink tongues. One coyote pup that had already been cleaned was off to one side, stopping to pounce on a grasshopper, the instinct to hunt already strong.

Murphy moved a few feet to the water's edge, feeling relaxed. She barked at her reflection, but the other dog didn't move, just stared back at her. Murphy drank hungrily from the icy water. Just a little bit further into the channel of water, white caps flowed swiftly past.

Murphy went to move back and lost her footing, slipping on the surface of a smooth, white rock, and landing on her side. *Ouch!*

She scampered back up and returned to take another lap of the cool, fresh water.

Suddenly there was a tussle, and a second later ferocious barking behind her. An eagle flew low, pausing just above ground to pick up the unattended pup, dangling it in its vise-like grip.

Mother swatted at the predator, trying to attack with the ferocity of a lion. She lunged at the bird, but tumbled down the riverbank a few feet before running right back up, her eyes never leaving her baby. When she leapt again, the mother splashed the water.

The eagle calmly, silently, began its ascent into the sky, the pup firmly held in its talons to head back to its nest to devour the meaty morsel.

Mother thrashed at the air again, one last attempt to free her pup, but knocked Murphy out of her way instead, and Murphy accidentally plunged back into the water, this time a little farther, into the icy current.

Murphy splashed, struggling to regain her balance. White caps swirled around her, propelling her downstream. The rapids carried Murphy away from the pack of coyotes, the only family she had. While the water wasn't particularly deep, it was shockingly cold. Murphy's legs bicycled quickly, but she couldn't find firm ground. Water began to fill her lungs and she struggled to breathe.

Chapter 33

Like all golden retrievers, Murphy had always loved the water. As soon as the Braun kids jumped in the family pool, they'd laugh and call, "Come on girl!" and she would jump in after them.

Murphy grew to love swimming so much she leaped fences for the refreshment, even in winter, much to the squeals and delight of the Braun children. Soon she started doing the same at other people's houses. She'd career off the pool fence, using it as a lever, and jump right in. Erin and Nathan apologized, but their hosts just laughed. It was as though Murphy couldn't be held back from having her very own party in the water.

"Murphy!" the kids would call and laugh. Nathan and Erin weren't quite as amused, but over time they got used to Murphy's water-loving ways and prepared for it by keeping her indoors when they didn't want her taking a swim.

Normally Murphy would be strong enough to get to the side and emerge from the water, but months in the wild had weakened her.

Struggling to keep her head afloat, the rest of Murphy's body thrashed under the surface. The natural instinct to paddle came easy, but Murphy wasn't swimming on her own terms. She'd never felt fear in the water before.

As Murphy cycled her legs, her heart pounded, the freezing water making it harder and harder to keep moving. Wild kicks grew slow as she silently sped down the uncharted water course. Her head bobbed above the frosty surface. She gulped water, her body banging against rocks and debris. She grew numb in the icy water. A landscape of trees whizzed by and just as Murphy's body began to surrender, she stopped. Water swirled all around her, yet she was held in place. A large branch in the water, a helping hand close to shore, had snagged her.

Using all of her remaining strength, Murphy crawled up the side and then staggered to dry land, her body dragging, scraping the earth. She lay down, sick and exhausted. Her sides ached as she heaved, throwing up much of the water she'd swallowed. She looked back at the river and for once a body of water didn't look like the party that had always beckoned her to join it.

Once again, Murphy was in a new place and completely on her own.

Chapter 34

Murphy walked back to the forest, where she felt most at ease. Armed with some tricks she'd learned from her time with the coyotes, she searched for an abandoned den to rest awhile.

Her ears perked up when she saw an upturned tree. It could be a spot to rest, where she wouldn't have to be on high alert as she'd grown so used to. With each passing week and then month in the wild, with each encounter that left Murphy nervous and fearful, she grew much more anxious than her old, relaxed self. She was also less trusting, suspicious of other living things. Instead of a healthy, soft coat, her fur had grown wiry and sparse in patches, the constant outdoor environment battering it. Instead of a few extra pounds from living an easy life with the Brauns, her frame was skinny, ribs beginning to protrude out her sides. The time in the wild was stripping Murphy's softness in form just as it was in character. For good reasons like enabling her to survive, and for bad—the constant fear—Murphy was getting tough.

She sniffed around the hole to investigate, but once she didn't sense any signs of life, Murphy burrowed her way in, leading with her nose just as the adult coyotes had shown her.

Ouch! A sharp pain shot through Murphy's jowls.

She let out a whine as she lunged for the attacker. It was a prickly animal with its own safety issues to worry about that inhabited the den. A porcupine had staved off Murphy's abrupt intrusion with a warning poke. But Murphy wasn't ready to back down. Her eyes glittered and her jaws clasped onto the animal's spiky hide. Murphy was quick to sink in her teeth.

Despite some pesky pokes, Murphy enjoyed the unexpected meal.

Afterward she slept deeply, a wonderful treat she could enjoy because of a full belly. Most of the time Murphy slept in spurts, her constant hunger an alarm clock she couldn't turn off.

Still, spring in the forest had its high and lows. The most important benefit was the abundance of food. Foliage and berries were plentiful, and animals came out of hibernation. Murphy especially enjoyed all of the yellow-bellied marmots, groundhog-like little critters. Murphy had become a skilled hunter of marmots, which she'd learned take little effort to find, since marmots practically give themselves away. If they were hiding in a hide-and-seek game, they'd lose every time. With their yellow bellies up, marmots were especially easy for Murphy to spot. Used to only a rare piece of meat during winter's scarcity, Murphy got her fill of marmots nearly every day that spring.

They dig holes in the ground for shelter, but they whistle, especially when they know they are in danger. If Murphy wasn't certain whether a marmot was burrowed in a hole, she would just wait for the inevitable whistling to start, then leap over and grab it.

One major downside to springtime is that the bears are wide awake. That spring Murphy found them well-rested and very, very hungry, which caused Murphy all kinds of grief. Whenever she stood near the water to find something to eat, a bear often appeared, bellowing at her to get away.

This was nothing new. It seemed Murphy was always escaping from one thing or another. Her once social personality changed to one that preferred to be reclusive. The more she was forced to flee from danger, the more fear became a part of who she had become.

When she'd sneak into a quiet campsite, drawn in by the intoxicating smells of barbecued ribs or fresh, grilled trout, more often than not something else had beaten her to it. Bears were always the gold medal winners in this race and did so without much effort. They just sat back, enjoying the chips, beef jerky, even scented lip balm, before Murphy had the chance to get to it first.

Soon the very sight of a bear brought something more irksome than fright: annoyance. Like a teased younger sibling, Murphy always felt like she was getting the door slammed on her. The bears calmly went about their business while she grew ever hungrier.

Chapter 35

Murphy watched a little, dark fish darting around, zig-zagging this way and that as if it wanted to be chased. The thought of playing was fleeting as hunger ruled Murphy at all times. As soon as she got close, ready to lunge, the fish moved away, zipping under the water. Murphy stood close, not splashing so that she could see her prey clearly. She lowered her head slowly, ready to take a chomp.

Another larger, silver fish cruised by, deeper out in the water. Murphy resisted her desire to stay safely on shore. She paused for a second, and then pushed her body into the water to tackle the larger fish, a salmon, enjoying the feel of it rushing in and then filling her mouth.

Murphy popped above the surface and splashed back to shore, locking the fish in her jaws as it thrashed back and forth while Murphy pushed forward up and then out. Once on firm ground Murphy trotted with her treasure, still firmly grasped, her exhaustion all but forgotten.

She dropped the fish to inspect it, but it smelled so fresh that Murphy had her jaw snapped around it at once, biting into the salmon's middle section. Bite after delicious bite, it was juicier than anything she'd eaten in a while, more satisfying than the various rodents she'd still been lucky enough to catch on occasion.

For the next few days Murphy remained by the water, finding it an easy place to hunt. If she remained still and kept her eyes laser-focused just below the river's surface, an unsuspecting fish was sure to come within her reach. Murphy no longer looked at the water as a place to play, but only as a place to work to get her next meal.

Murphy felt fuller, and slept better, than she had in weeks.

Chapter 36

Murphy was just beginning to snooze, half of a fish she hadn't finished still by her side, when she heard a growl and sprang to attention. A large cat, a mountain lion, hissed viciously, just inches from her head.

The mountain lion looked down and snatched the fish for her own meal, just as a rude child grabs food off another person's plate. The large cat retreated as quickly as she had come, carrying the glittering, silver prize in her mouth. She turned back to stare at Murphy as she walked up the bank to higher ground for a nice place to relax and enjoy her picnic, perched above all. Her eyes bore into Murphy's until Murphy looked away. She sensed danger and understood that this stranger was not her friend.

The mountain lion remained in Murphy's

territory, a permanent fixture perched high above the riverbed. Sometimes she would disappear from view for a while, but then come right back, reigning over the area, gazing straight ahead, strong and serious.

It was a particularly slow fishing day. As Murphy sniffed moist dirt, a few feet from the river's edge, something tan flashed into her side view. Before her next breath, Murphy was knocked to the ground, the large cat's paws gripping Murphy's slight frame, just as the large cat opened her mouth to reveal bared teeth, hurrying to take her first bite.

With bony ribs exposed on her faded gold coat, Murphy didn't look like much of a fighter. She was tired and not much surprised her anymore. But then something miraculous happened. The mountain lion paused for one instant to change her attack angle and in that one breath, just before she could go in for the kill, Murphy was able to break free. Her aching body sprang backward, full of adrenaline and desperation, and then lurched into the face of the snapping, hungry beast. The mountain lion's golden eyes stared shiny and fierce. After her own share of lean meals in recent days, she had grown impatient and wanted nothing more than to make Murphy her next meal.

Now that she was fueled by courage, the instinct to run away took over. Murphy rushed toward the river. Danger would be waiting wherever she went. Murphy didn't want to go into the water, where she'd be out of control; but if she turned back toward the mountain lion, that meant certain death. Just before she made contact with the water, Murphy pushed off the muddy ground as the mountain lion gave chase. The mountain lion was quicker. As Murphy pushed up a small hill, a sharp pain shot through her neck, slamming her to the ground, rendering her immobile. The mountain lion had Murphy in her grip and would be sure not to let her go this time. She whipped Murphy back and forth like a ragdoll, until her weak and defenseless body went still. Suddenly, the lion dropped Murphy, leaving her in shock and uncertain what to do. The cat whipped away, hissing menacingly. She appeared to be yelling, "Get away from me!"

A bear was inches away. He rose on his hind legs as he boasted his strength, the heat of his hot breath on them. "Rooooaaaaarrrrrr!"

The mountain lion moved in a third direction, away from both Murphy and the bear. Murphy took the chance to run away from both intruders.

When she finally stopped to rest she licked her paws, battered and sore. As she became more and more famished, Murphy was compelled to go back to the river, back to where she might find food. She was distracted by fresh green blades of grass, pausing to nibble patches of it.

Once she had ambled back to the water, Murphy looked up to see if the hungry mountain lion would be up high, gazing at everything in the open space from her pedestal on a towering rock. Murphy could see nothing on the rock or near it. For the time being, the mountain lion was nowhere to be seen.

At dusk, Murphy dozed until a pulling sound interrupted her reverie. Something was being dragged, sliding heavily along the ground. Murphy raised her head to see the same nonchalant bear she had encountered earlier, only this time it was very busy, dragging the lifeless, floppy body of the mountain lion from the area.

Murphy watched the bear retreat to the forest, dragging the once-fierce animal. When Murphy didn't hear any noise or movement, she felt safe to get back to her favorite pastime: fishing.

Chapter 37

Summer, 2013

Campers returned, filling the campsites, bringing more opportunities for Murphy to eat. On Sunday nights garbage cans overflowed with tossed out leftovers. Murphy scored fruit, graham crackers, and if she was lucky, a leftover hamburger or some other treat a small child couldn't finish.

There was more food, but also more frustrations for Murphy to navigate. More animals came out to compete for the food humans left unsecured or just hastily left behind. Just as before, however, many riches were being picked over by bears before Murphy had a chance to get to them. A half-eaten apple, dropped by a hiker and then inadvertently kicked in the dirt until disguised, shined bright to hungry animals. Someone's trash is someone else's treasure. A war would ensue for such a tasty object.

Chapter 38

Everything was still and calm, just the way Murphy liked it. She saw a large, triangular-shaped green tent and walked tentatively toward it, hoping a food source would be inside. As she drew near, Murphy sniffed under and then next to the picnic table, taking in something that was smoky—or was it meat? Just as she raised her nose, sniffing the air, a noise startled her. She jerked her head up, quickly coming to attention. A woman let out a surprised gasp, a baby snuggled to her chest, while pointing at Murphy. The look in her eyes wasn't the warm, adoring one Murphy had been accustomed to long ago. The person's eyes certainly did not convey delight, but shock and confusion. The feelings were mutual, and Murphy turned to run.

The humans Murphy encountered by then almost always thought she was a wild animal, with no place to call home and no one to care for her. Truthfully, the notion wasn't so far-fetched. Murphy had to fend for herself to survive. Having grown used to isolation, the feelings of fear were reciprocal. She would always hide in the woods for her own safety. And for anyone who may have wanted to give her a chance, to stop and see why she was all alone, those people never had the opportunity.

If she did come across the rare hiker who tried to check if she had a collar, or who did have kind eyes and a soothing voice, Murphy still ran away. Too often she had learned that each encounter meant a divide, some sort of conflict where she would rarely came out the winner.

With each scream of panic, each loud voice telling her to "Go!" with finger pointed, Murphy understood that she wasn't wanted. Murphy's reflexes to come close for a cuddle, a pat, or a kind word had been erased long before.

When her stomach was full, or at least satisfied, Murphy could rest, but she was always cautious, always aware of her surroundings.

When she grew to know a location and its routines she felt more at ease. She felt most comfortable when she could stay in the same place for a while. Still, Murphy's stomach was her leader. When it grumbled, Murphy walked on in the forest. She'd investigate new surroundings by sniffing, sometimes leading her to a few nibbles on bushes. When her stomach really hollered, Murphy would often be left to crunch on nothing but fallen branches.

Early one morning, Murphy risked going back to the campsites. She couldn't stand the tempting smells any longer. She had sniffed the air and grew ravenous from the aromas—sweet, salty, steaming, and spicy. Uncertain where it would lead her, Murphy would allow the strongest of smells to be her guide.

It is always better to lead by the head and not by what we want, but as a dog, Murphy was always led by her stomach first. She walked straight to a picnic table, sniffing the ground around it, smelling something that had spilled on the bar base, and began to lick.

The sweet flavor captivated Murphy. It flooded her senses and made her relax. She wasn't paying attention to her surroundings, but suddenly, Murphy realized she wasn't alone.

A slamming noise interrupted Murphy's simple, sticky pleasure and she yanked her head up. Another dog was running from the clanking of a silver pet bowl. The dog had undoubtedly been doing the same thing at the campsite Murphy was, trolling for a half-eaten granola bar or for a dish of dog food—whatever it could find. Murphy saw the other dog, but the dog didn't see her.

Though she could see no other signs of life, a slight, smoldering fire that still burned caught her eye at a campsite across the way. Murphy watched the smoke, a visible wafting trail, and sniffed the smoky richness in the air as she walked closer.

She let her guard down a bit, focusing on the hypnotizing smell. Murphy continued to move toward it when—*Ouch*! Something pierced her side! The jolting pain was searing, making it nearly impossible for Murphy to walk. She limped away hurriedly, retreating into the forest, the only sure place she knew. On the other side of the campsite a teenage boy slung a pellet gun over his shoulder as a wave of adrenaline washed over him.

The boy knew his parents would be mad if they knew he was shooting at animals, but his curiosity had gotten the better of him. Being curious was not a reason to aim and shoot. The boy was certain he had aimed correctly and believed he had struck something because of the quick flash of movement he saw when he shot, but when he walked toward the spot, there was nothing.

Murphy walked on in the thick brush of forest, no campsites or people to be seen, as she searched for an empty den in which to rest and take shelter. It was a strategy she had learned from her time with the coyotes.

As morning morphed into early afternoon, the sun was still held at bay, its rays not able to penetrate the forest's thick cloak. Murphy loped through the woods, her side aching and her mouth dry, when the smell of smoke grabbed her attention once again. She sniffed the air, trying to collect clues, when a bird flew just next to her in a terrible hurry. A mouse and two squirrels hurried past as well. Within seconds, more birds, mice, and other rodents rushed toward Murphy, a miniature stampede, but they didn't stop or even take notice of her presence. They seemed more fearful of what was behind them than what a much bigger animal like Murphy could do to them. More and more animals scampered right on past, leaving Murphy glued to her spot, watching them parade past.

One animal wasn't strong enough to escape whatever it was they were all fleeing from, however. A tiny, gray bird had fallen, defenseless. Murphy snatched the shocked and injured bird in her jaws as the other animals continued to stream past her, and ate it hurriedly so that she, too, could follow the crowd away from the smoky drama.

Chapter 39

Fall, 2013

A full year, and all four seasons in the forest, came and went. As the leaves turned red, purple, and orange, the granite peaks became dusted with light snow. As the temperature dropped, the bears in the forest hurried to fill their stomachs for another wintry rest. They particularly enjoyed acorns, apples, and manzanita berries.

Warm summer days in the forest gave way to cool ones, and the nights were downright brisk.

Murphy may not have been aware that the one-year anniversary since she went missing passed, but the Brauns solemnly marked the occasion back at home. They struggled with the word *anniversary,* because that word should really be used for happy occasions, like wedding anniversaries.

As soon as campers began to pack up their gear and leave the area for the season, Murphy's nocturnal food prizes went with them, forcing her to endure frequent hunger once more.

One crisp, late afternoon, United States Army Veteran Drake Murphy drove from his home in El Dorado County to French Meadows in the Tahoe National Forest, one of his favorite places in the forest to escape from the outside world. It was only out in nature that Drake could forget his problems, at least for a little while.

Drake had traveled all over the world when he served in the military, but after being honorably discharged he chose to move back to El Dorado County, where he'd been born and raised. During his travels, he came to realize he preferred home and didn't think anywhere in the world was as beautiful as Gold Country (as it's lovingly nicknamed). His rural county was full of rivers, lakes, streams, waterfalls, and, of course, the region's jewel, Lake Tahoe.

He'd always enjoyed the four seasons living in this part of California. The summers are hot, the winters are cold, and fall and spring are mild and colorful; some say the area even rivals the east coast's plethora of autumn colors.

Most of the cities and unincorporated towns in El Dorado County are rural, but if Drake ever wanted to visit a big city, Sacramento was close and San Francisco was only a few hours' drive west.

He was only 27 years old, but Drake had already experienced more than men twice his age have. Sometimes, he even thought he'd seen more than most people have in a lifetime.

Drake had been home from serving for almost two years overseas, recuperating after surviving an attack in Afghanistan during the War on Terror. An explosion mangled one of his legs. In order to save his life, doctors had no choice but to remove it. They had said that at worst he'd be in a wheelchair for the rest of his life. At best, he'd have to learn to walk with a prosthetic leg.

After the injury, everyone told Drake how lucky he had been because the doctors hadn't been sure he would survive. Drake knew he was lucky, too, but that didn't ease the constant pain. It robbed him of the spunk he'd always had, the spirit that had begun to fade even before his injury because of all he'd seen during war. The explosion had only finished the job.

While recovering, Drake wanted nothing more than to get out of his wheelchair. When he was fitted for his prosthetic leg, he just wanted to walk as he had before, without a limp. As little children stared at him and then whispered to their mothers, who hushed them, then offered a quick, apologetic smile, Drake would think about how he'd always taken something as simple as going for a run, let alone a walk, for granted.

There were many things he didn't appreciate before his injury, but Drake still couldn't help but think life had been easier back then.

No matter what his condition, Drake was strengthened in the knowledge that he wouldn't have changed anything about his choice to enlist to serve his country. He certainly had no regrets about that.

He'd been a high school student on September 11, 2001. He'd woken that morning to learn that two airplanes had purposely flown into the World Trade Center's Twin Towers in New York City. Drake may have been a kid, but he seethed as he understood that America's freedoms were at risk and that it was the enemies' wish to annihilate the American Dream.

When American troops were sent to the Middle East soon afterward, Drake couldn't shake the feeling that he should be there, too. The feeling only grew stronger.

Instead of thinking about which colleges he should apply to, Drake couldn't get the idea out of his head that he needed to serve his country and protect its freedoms.

"Mom, Dad—I want to enlist," he told his parents one day. "I want to join the Army."

His parents were surprised. They had watched their son grow from a little boy who had to be reminded to do simple chores, like make his bed or empty the dishwasher, transform into a young man who was choosing to dedicate his life to his country.

And that was just the beginning.

Once he enlisted, Drake would change from an awkward teenager into a man who looked others in the eye confidently as he shook their hands.

He went from watching television late into the night and sleeping in on weekends, to a focused young man who rose early to exercise. Muscles began to appear on Drake's arms, back, and legs that he didn't even know he had. He had transformed from a gawky boy who walked with a slight slouch to a strong young man who stood tall and proud. He would run miles every day, first during Basic Training, but he kept it up, running right up until the day he couldn't run anymore.

The dirty blond hair that had previously flopped over his eyes and hid his ears had been cut short and clean.

While serving in the military had changed Drake for the better, it wasn't without its drawbacks. War changed him on the inside as well as the outside.

Before he left for Afghanistan, Drake's biggest worry was whether his family's orchard was free from brush and pests. People from all over the state and beyond traveled to his family's business to buy blueberries, apples, pumpkins, and Christmas trees.

He had spent his life helping with the family business, but once he came home he woke up each day in pain.

The morning of his catastrophic injury had started off just like any other day. The men in Drake's unit had bonded as brothers. They spent their free time together, doing things like working out, shooting hoops, playing football, playing pranks on each other, or just watching movies. A few of the guys had even formed a band. Whatever they were doing, it always included talking about their lives back home. After breakfast that hot, summer morning, Drake had been playing cards with his bunkmate, Beau Allen, from Alabama.

Then Drake left for security patrol just north of Afghanistan's capital city, Kabul. As civilians bustled to buy, sell, or trade at a marketplace, Drake stood still, studying it, peering closely as he scanned the crowd and the clusters of people moving within it to see if anything seemed unusual. Just as his eyes began to feel heavy, Drake heard a scuffle to his left, and then a loud shout.

In the same second, a deafening explosion slammed Drake to the ground.

Excruciating pain shot through his shattered legs, taking his breath away. His eyes stared ahead as he struggled to take tiny gasps of air. When even the sight of things caused him pain, Drake closed his eyes.

He would later learn that doctors would have to remove his right leg, which had been twisted in the explosion, from the hip down in order to save his life.

He would also discover that he had been one of the lucky ones. Two of his Army brothers, including Beau, and 14 innocent Afghan civilians, died that day because of one person's actions.

Chapter 40

After weeks, and then months, recovering in an Army hospital, Drake was finally able to go home.

People from all over the United States wrote him letters and thanked him for his service. He also received a Purple Heart—a prestigious military medal awarded to American service men and women who are wounded or killed while serving their country.

Even after being fitted with a prosthetic leg, Drake still felt pain and he would always walk with a limp. The pain he felt and the memories, particularly from the day of the accident, were what made Drake feel depressed about his changed life sometimes. The final sting was that his girlfriend, whom he'd planned to marry, didn't wait for him. She had come to visit in the beginning, but then something changed in her eyes. Before long, she didn't come at all.

"She doesn't deserve you," his mother would say. "She wasn't the one."

Despite all of it, Drake knew he would enlist all over again if he were given the chance. The feelings he expressed to his parents about wanting to serve his country had only grown stronger over the years. Not being there to stand side by side with his Army brothers hurt even more than the physical pain in his leg.

Back at camp it was after dusk and Drake looked up at the brightening stars, thinking about the various medical appointments he had that week. A dull pain he had grown accustomed to persisted, radiating throughout his hip. He breathed in, focusing on the fresh, mountain air.

There was a rustle by an empty fire pit across the way. The metal grate over the fire had been plunked to one side. An animal darted away from the sound, dodging to get away.

Drake's heart thumped. The animal looked like a coyote, tan-gold and very thin.

It's just doing what it has to do to survive, Drake thought. He kept staring, squinting to get a closer look at the animal. The shape of its face and its tail looked like a dog's.

That's no coyote, Drake thought. He put down his silver tumbler of coffee. In his left hand, he held a roast beef deli sandwich.

"Come here, boy," Drake clucked. He picked up a flashlight and shined the light in Murphy's direction.

Murphy, not used to a kind tone, stopped. She looked back, seeing a flicker of light across the way. It seemed to be welcoming and warm, just like the voice. She'd missed the gentle pats of grownups and the playfulness of little children. Life in the wild had been many things, but it was always lonely and tiresome.

Drake held out the sandwich. "Are you hungry, boy?" he said again, assuming, as most people do, that any new animal is male.

Drake tore off a piece of the sandwich and threw it a little farther out, an offering of friendship and a promise of peace. Murphy limped a few steps, still unsure of her safety, then stopped, still thirty feet away.

"Come on, boy," Drake repeated, moving the glaring light from Murphy and shining it on the sandwich instead. Murphy walked toward him slowly, her mouth already watering from the sight and smell of the sandwich.

Murphy's heart raced as she encountered this new person, but her hunger was too strong. Once she was close enough for Drake to reach out and pet her if he wanted to, Murphy sniffed the chunk of sandwich and, quickly determining it passed inspection, gulped it down.

She looked up at Drake, whose eyes were kind and whose voice was just as reassuring.

"What's happened to you, friend?" Drake asked, reaching his hand out to Murphy.

She reluctantly walked toward it.

How often had she been surprised in similar moments? Right when she'd get close to someone or something new, she always received a poke or a hiss or a frightening growl.

Murphy was ready to flee at any second when Drake began to rub her head, right where she liked it—between the ears. She stayed, wanting to feel the relaxation for at least a little while.

Drake inspected Murphy all over, front to back, and felt around her neck for a collar or for any identifying mark.

"Someone must be missing you," he said, his voice to Murphy as comforting as the gentle massaging motions he made with his hands on Murphy's neck. Her stiff, defensive pose slowly began to relax, but not completely.

Drake carefully rose and began to build a fire, his leg stiff from sitting so long. He scooped some of the chili he had heated onto a piece of cardboard for Murphy. It may not have been fancy, but it was the first kind of dish she'd eaten from in a year. Dish or no dish, Murphy wolfed the warm food down hungrily and then started to dig in to the cardboard, licking any remaining bit of salty, meaty goodness she could from it.

"I see you're hungry," Drake observed as he bent down to scoop another lump onto the frayed cardboard.

He sat down again.

Man and dog remained by the fire together as new friends.

Later that night Drake lowered the tailgate of his truck and climbed up into the bed. He loved sleeping under the stars. A sleeping bag and mat made it very comfortable. He beckoned for Murphy to join him, but Murphy stayed on the ground.

Drake shifted his body around and just before he decided to remove his prostheses for the night, he had a thought. He got back out of the truck, only this time with the ramp he used with his wheelchair. He positioned it so that Murphy could walk up it if she wanted to.

Perhaps her hips hurt, Drake thought, realizing earlier in the evening that his new friend is female.

Yet Murphy remained glued to her spot, even when Drake got out of the truck and took Murphy by the scruff of her neck. "Come on, girl," he said. Murphy shuffled a few steps up the ramp, the soothing tone of Drake's voice the only reason she walked into the unknown space. She laid down close to the edge, ready to jump and run should she need to. But as her eyes grew heavy, Murphy didn't feel the urge to run. Her belly was full and she felt safe. Soon Murphy surrendered to sleep.

Her peaceful slumber didn't last long. In the darkness as Drake slept, she heard a noise. Drake snored loudly and Murphy opened her eyes, ready to run. She remained on guard the rest of the night.

The next morning, the thick thistles in Murphy's

fur were more evident. As they sat together by the smoky morning fire, Drake worked to remove them, one by one. Murphy flinched, but would gladly endure it for the chunks of fried egg and stick of beef jerky that she now enjoyed. Drake happily shared all of the food he had packed with his new buddy.

After breakfast Drake walked to a spigot to collect water in a pot. Murphy watched as Drake limped, carrying the heavy pot to set it on the grate over the fire. In another pot filled with water he added a colorful liquid, which Murphy could smell from a distance, but that didn't smell like something she'd like to eat. As soon as he poured the liquid in, billows of white foam seeped up and nearly over the sides.

"Time for a bath," Drake said. The night before he could barely sleep because the dog smelled so bad. "Come."

Murphy stood still, cowering. As he had done each time Drake wanted Murphy to do something, he gently pulled her by the scruff of her neck. Murphy's body was tense, but she hesitantly moved with Drake.

He reached into the pot and began rubbing soapy water all over Murphy's dirty sides. She wagged her tail and tried licking the water, but it tasted bitter. As Drake moved his hands and the sudsy massage up to Murphy's head, she closed her eyes, basking in the wonderful feeling, opening her mouth to smile and wagging her tail.

Drake intermittently poured warm water over her

to clear the soap suds off her fur. Although she was clean for the first time in a year, her patchy fur would have been unrecognizable to those who had known her. Murphy's formerly deep red fur had been bleached whitish-yellow from the months she had spent outdoors, under the heat of the unrelenting sun.

Instinctively, Murphy shook the water off of her coat with all her might, doing the job of drying herself that Drake never had a chance to start.

"Aaaaaa!" Drake yelled in surprise as the water drenched him. Murphy startled and stopped at the loud sound, her tail between her legs, and looked at Drake despairingly.

"It's okay, girl," Drake assured her. "It's okay."

As he looked into her eyes and rubbed her neck, Murphy's fear dissipated a bit.

Chapter 41

Once the sky turned black and millions of stars lit up the sky, Drake settled in to the bed of the truck, wrapping the sleeping bag around his body. He was too tired to coax Murphy in with him; plus she looked content where she was. He figured she would be fine, and she was, until later that night.

Murphy woke from a light sleep and walked to the pit where the fire had burned so brightly before, looking for the small flap of a box that served as her food dish. She was still hungry, and thought she might find some leftovers.

A loud, vicious hiss stopped Murphy cold. An opossum snarled at her from just a few feet away. It was holding the softened cardboard tightly in its grip, and then it slunk off into the darkness with Murphy's dish.

Murphy took off after it. She single-mindedly gave chase to the intruder, scrambling to catch it. Heart racing, she had forgotten the peace that Drake had worked so hard to achieve in a second as she quickly jumped back into the only mode she'd grown to know: survival.

When Drake woke up in the morning, Murphy was gone.

Chapter 42

January, 2014

Winter days grew cold and short. Darkness became more familiar than daylight. Two hours west, as the wind whipped and rain fell in the foothills, the Brauns knew it meant that snow was falling in the mountains and in the forest. Yet, even with some rain, it was still a milder winter than most. While the rest of the state prayed for more rain during California's historic drought, the dryer than normal weather gave the Brauns hope that Murphy was surviving.

They never stopped sharing stories about Murphy. Matthew and Morgan still talked about Murphy every day. While at first they asked when she would be home, now they asked whether or not she would.

Finegan was the only one in the family who had stopped asking, which was only natural. By then Finegan was nearly three years old and had spent more time without Murphy in his life than with her in it. However, when he saw a picture of Murphy, he instantly touched it and said, "Murph."

Chapter 43

In order to find food, she'd grown accustomed to looking for the clues that pikas leave behind. Murphy knew that if she saw a branch sticking out of a burrow, it meant that delicious meat was near.

The first time Murphy caught a porcupine had been a surprise. Now she knew to creep up stealthily, and use her paws to flip the prickly rodent on its back to save herself from the quills, the only thing they used to defend themselves. Then Murphy would attack the rodent's soft underbelly. She was still pierced by quills occasionally, even when Murphy thought her method of attack was assured. As soon as she dived in to surprise her prey, the porcupine got one last stab at Murphy, grazing her eye with its pointed weapon. Murphy cried out in pain. Yet even with a stinging eye that was quickly swelling shut, she continued to attack and her victory was in getting the meal that would ensure her survival for another day.

The pika and porcupine meat would sustain Murphy for a little while, but soon hunger would come knocking as it always did, bothering her so much that she couldn't sleep.

She walked through the forest, nibbling at exposed pieces of bark, dried twigs, and leaves, an inch of snow dusting them. She heard the familiar sound of a pika cry, but it wasn't crystal clear; it was muffled.

A small animal that looked like a miniature version of a brown bear had its hind quarters up, reaching deep into a burrow from where the sound originated. Only this was no bear. The largest in the weasel family, the elusive wolverine was attacking a pika family. It emerged from the burrow with meat in its mouth, one unlucky member of the family in its grasp, as the wolverine meandered in Murphy's direction.

Murphy shielded herself from view behind a tree as she watched the powerful animal devour the rest of the now-silent, tiny rabbit. The wolverine left no trace as it ate every last bit of it, teeth and all.

Murphy's sense of fear around the animal was strong. She stood back, in awe of the bold and ferocious beast.

It wouldn't be the only time Murphy would see a wolverine that winter. One day Murphy came upon a deer that had been killed some time before, most likely attacked and eaten by another animal that couldn't finish so much meat in one sitting. By the time Murphy found the deer its carcass was frozen and the meat hard to chew, but Murphy worked away at it, happy for anything she could get. Her mouth stinging from the cold, Murphy dropped a piece of the frozen meat. Just then something rustled above her, but paying no mind, Murphy kept gnawing away.

Suddenly, she noticed something fall to the ground just behind her. Long sharp claws on full display, the wolverine rushed at Murphy, losing its footing for a second, and then easily maneuvering through the snow that Murphy had found so slippery. Eyes wide, it lunged toward Murphy and her feast.

The wolverine snarled at Murphy as she backed away from what was left of the deer. The cold was just a minor irritant to the savage wolverine. While the meat stung her mouth, making it almost impossible to chew, the wolverine ate the meat ravenously, paying no mind to its tough, frozen texture.

She walked away from the deer and wolverine to search for a resting place. Although she gladly would have eaten more, she was ready to give up the food she so badly desired to the intruder. She soon found a hollowed out tree trunk that was large enough for her to crawl into. Murphy closed her eyes and besides the hunger in her belly that made it hard to rest, exhaustion was stronger. Murphy wanted nothing more than to surrender to sleep.

Chapter 44

June, 2014

It was a beautiful, late spring morning. A man and woman were driving their Jeep close to the French Meadows Reservoir. The man stopped suddenly when he noticed an emaciated, pale yellow dog just a stone's throw away, staring at them.

"Hey there," the man said, stretching out his arm to offer his hand, feeling safe to do so from inside his vehicle. Yet they didn't get the chance to investigate. The dog ran in the opposite direction and into the woods, but not before meeting the man's eyes. He saw a flash of sadness before the animal disappeared.

"It's amazing that such a sick-looking animal could move so fast," the man said to the woman.

After nearly two years many of the Brauns'

missing dog posters were tattered or gone, but their contact information popped up first when the man entered these words into a search engine: "Lost golden retriever, Placer County, El Dorado County."

He dialed the first number that resulted from the search on his cell phone.

On the other end, Nathan answered the call. When the man explained that he had seen a dog who might be Murphy, Nathan was skeptical.

"Are you sure it was a golden retriever?"' he asked.

"Yes, I'm sure of it," the man replied. "I wasn't going to call, but something told me to."

"Could you tell if it was a boy or a girl?" Nathan asked.

"I'm not sure," the man said.

"What did the dog do when you approached it?" Nathan asked.

"It looked at me closely for a second and then it turned away really fast in the opposite direction," the caller explained.

"What color is your Jeep?" Nathan asked, thinking about his own white Jeep, wondering if perhaps this dog might have thought it was him. He quickly shut down the thought, not wanting to get his hopes up again.

"White," the man said.

Nathan's palms grew sweaty and his heart beat faster.

Chapter 45

Right after Murphy was lost they had received one to two calls a day, then one or two a week. After nearly two years the Brauns were lucky if they got one or two sighting calls a month.

It was peculiar that within a few days that spring there was an increase in sighting calls. Each of the callers had seen what appeared to be a lost golden retriever in French Meadows, an area about five miles as the crow flies, from where Nathan had last seen Murphy.

He hung up the phone and told Erin about what the man with the white Jeep had said.

They decided to call their veterinarian. "If this really was Murphy, what might she be like now? Would she behave like a feral animal?" Erin asked.

"If it *was* Murphy, she is looking for you and

wants to be home," the vet said. "She is fighting to stay alive and just wants to find her family. She wouldn't have forgotten about you."

If at first Nathan had felt unsure what to do, after hearing these words, he and Erin were certain.

"You need to go camping," Erin urged, seconds before Nathan could say he was packing up his Jeep with camping gear.

As soon as Bubba and Larry heard the news, they were ready to go with their best friend. The three men and Matthew headed to Ahart campgrounds in the French Meadows reservoir region, equipped with eight pounds of bacon and an even bigger bag of dog food.

Not wanting to tell Matthew the real reason behind the trip, Nathan tried playing cool at first, acting as though it were one of their regular trips, only they didn't need to go off-roading to get there.

Nathan concealed the handmade lost dog signs he had made, but once they arrived at camp his exhilaration was evident.

"Murphy!" he shouted from the driver's seat, unleashing all of the worry and all of the hope he held inside simultaneously.

"Why are you calling Murphy, Dad?" Matthew asked, eyes wide, wanting to be let in on any news. The kids used to ask if there were any leads every day, sometimes multiple times a day, but by then they only asked for information when Murphy's name came up or when they'd see other golden retrievers.

Seeing another golden retriever used to make them think of Murphy in a happy way; now Erin and Nathan couldn't help but turn away when they'd see one. Sometimes they could be having a perfectly fine day, but seeing another golden playing fetch, or smiling at her family as she was out for a walk in the neighborhood, could bring on a stomach ache that hurt so bad it was more like heart ache.

"I don't know," Nathan stammered, staring ahead at the road. "When we're out here…you just never know."

As Nathan pulled his truck up to the gate, the campground host was there to greet them.

"How long you staying?" the host asked as Nathan reached for his wallet.

"Hopefully one night so we can get our dog and get out of here," Nathan replied, counting his cash.

Nathan paused and looked up at the man. "I'm looking for our golden retriever we lost 20 months ago."

Then speaking more slowly, he lowered his voice. "I've heard there's been a golden sighting here."

The host, Jason Smith, stopped searching for a map to give them and looked Nathan in the eye.

"I know exactly what you're talking about," he said. "There's a dog going from campsite to campsite. I see it every three days or so, looking around the campsites for anything to eat." Nathan had never heard sweeter words. Mouth open, he listened in astonishment.

"I put food and water out for it, but I never actually see it eating or drinking," Jason continued. "But the next morning, the bowls are empty."

Jason looked beyond Nathan out into the limitless forest, gesturing with his arms where the mysterious dog might be. "Some people think it's a coyote, but I'm positive it's a dog. I haven't seen it in a few days, so it should be back anytime…maybe tonight or this weekend."

Those words were like fuel to Nathan's soul. He perked right up. Nathan couldn't shield his excitement from Matthew, or from himself for that matter. Like a whistling tea pot, he began to shake at his core. In 20 months, nearly two years, there hadn't been a sighting that had given him any reason to believe Murphy was still alive, searching for a way to come home, just as they had doggedly searched for her.

Matthew, who had been resting in the back seat, was sitting up, eyes wide.

Jason gave them a map of the campgrounds and circled the vicinity where he'd last seen the elusive dog that might be Murphy. Nathan chose the closest campsite, which was still available. Even if no sites had been available, there was no turning back now. Nathan would do anything, pay anything, to spend just one night with the hope that Murphy might find her way back to them.

Before the truck engine cooled Nathan and Larry were already out, frying all the bacon they brought to lure Murphy. There was a couple at the camp site right next to them and they couldn't help but notice the men wasted no time to cook. The smell of bacon wafted over to their site.

"Must be hungry," they said, eyebrows raised, to one another.

The couple went for a walk to see who these curious campers were the ones who cooked all that bacon before they'd even pitched a tent. Nathan glanced up and, catching their eyes, smiled.

"What's up?" the man asked.

As Nathan cooked, he wasted no time sharing their story. *The more eyes looking out for Murphy the better,* he thought.

"Maybe it's not so unrealistic that your dog's still alive," the woman said.

Nathan stood taller when he heard this, relishing every word.

"Yeah, we come up here to snowmobile every winter," the man continued. "But the past two winters have been so mild, with such little snow, we haven't been able to…Maybe a dog *could* survive out here."

Nathan still wanted to protect himself from disappointment. He had heard so many stories that had given him hope, but they still hadn't brought Murphy home. Still, he couldn't quiet the voice in his head that excitedly asked, "Could it really be?"

He begrudgingly packed up the bacon. The last thing they needed was for a bear to pay them a visit.

That night Nathan could barely sleep as he waited for Murphy to walk through the campsite. It was a long night of tossing and turning. Every noise gave him a start.

When they finally woke to birds chirping and the sun magnifying everything inside their tent, Matthew realized that Murphy had never come. He stumbled outside the tent and didn't see her.

"Let's pack up," Nathan said, already up, sitting in a chair by the extinguished camp fire, a cup of steaming coffee in his hand.

He had one more idea before they'd leave, however; one last try to let Murphy know they were near and that it was safe to show herself.

The men and Matthew threw a few things in the back of the truck and made the short drive back to Jason Smith's trailer.

Jason was already out front, getting ready to jump in his own truck to patrol the sites.

"Hey Jason," Nathan called as he swung one leg out of the truck. The others stayed inside.

"Could I leave a couple of things with you to put out for our dog, just in case she comes back?" Nathan asked, walking toward Jason.

"You bet," he answered.

Besides bacon, Nathan knew exactly what familiar smells might entice Murphy. He took off his worn baseball cap and handed it to Jason. He turned to the truck and pulled out an old blanket, draping it over his shoulder, and then heaved a 20 pound bag of dog food over his head.

"Sure that's enough?" Jason laughed, gladly accepting the goods.

Nathan searched his mind to decide if there was anything else he could do. He'd give the whole world if he could. He'd give anything to bring Murphy home.

Thank goodness we didn't go on that trip, Nathan thought. He and Erin had had plans to get out of town for a week with the kids, but something told Nathan not to go. In that moment, he was glad he had listened to his intuition.

"There's too much going on," they had explained to the kids about the change in plans.

He wasn't sure at the time, but now he knew.

What if I'd missed the call, the most promising call we've had yet? Nathan thought.

Everything was fitting together as perfectly as a puzzle, beginning with his and Erin's intuition that Nathan should go camping to follow the fellow Jeeper's lost dog description. Still, there was a missing piece to the puzzle, one that left a gaping hole, a void that would only be filled by Murphy's homecoming.

Chapter 46

It was a quiet evening, with only the raccoons to battle for food. For this reason, Murphy walked into a campsite that had a brightly colored tablecloth draped across a bolted down picnic table. A beverage container teetered on the table's edge, perilously close to toppling over. Murphy went toward it, hopeful for a drink, even for a drop.

A familiar scent caught Murphy's attention, making her think of a time long ago. She thought of their cuddles, their kisses, and the food that peppered their kitchen floor while Erin was cooking. Murphy turned toward the smell, and with it, the memories. She lost interest in the camping table or what she might find there. Her nose pointed up and twitched in the air.

She was captivated by the scent that she hadn't

experienced in the forest until now. She was still wary of her surroundings, wary of getting caught or being attacked by another animal. She crept to the road and away from the campsite with caution as the smell grew stronger, unavoidable by the time she saw something lying on the side of the road. Murphy preferred to stay hidden, stealthy, enshrouded by trees, yet the mound of fabric, a soft nest that emanated the best smell in the world to her, was too alluring. She walked tentatively toward it and, upon reaching it, laid down at once, memories rushing over her of an easier life when she was loved and cared for.

Instead of being on guard, with every muscle and tendon ready to fight, Murphy relaxed, closed her eyes, and instantly fell asleep on the cap and blanket.

Sometime later a voice interrupted her. "Psst!" was the sound, startling Murphy awake. She was still resting comfortably on top of the blanket, her head resting on Nathan's baseball cap. A man and a woman stood on either side of her. When Murphy stood up to run away, the man grabbed her by the scruff of her neck and wouldn't let go. Murphy resisted and squirmed to get away.

"Sit," the man said, and she did. It was a command that Murphy hadn't heard in a long time, but instinctively she knew what to do.

"You stay," he commanded again, firmer now. Murphy stood up to go, but she met resistance against the man's grasp. She continued to struggle.

The woman walked over and knelt down. She

opened a steel cage, something that equated to prison to Murphy, and tried to coax the dog to go inside using a treat. Murphy wouldn't be tempted. She crouched down, digging her paws into the dusty ground and remained anchored to her spot.

Pointing at Murphy as he kept one eye on her the man, Jason Smith, again said, "Stay." He slowly began to walk the few steps to his truck to grab a rope to use as a leash. As soon as he was one foot further than he could grab her, Murphy ran.

"What's going on?" a nearby camper called, overhearing the ruckus. "Wild animal?"

"Naw, I think that was someone's lost dog," Jason replied. "They've been looking all over for her. I told them I'd hold her if she came by."

The camper looked in the direction where Murphy had gone.

"I saw her before I had a chance to grab a leash," Jason said. "Crazy dog...she doesn't know how much better her life would be if she'd just come back."

Chapter 47

Saturday, June 15, 2014

Little did the Brauns know that the impossible would happen on a day that started with a groggy wake-up call. Nathan went through the motions to pick up the ringing phone before his brain registered what he was doing.

"Hello?" he grumbled, still asleep.

"Nathan Braun?" a man at the other end of the phone asked.

"Yes," Nathan said, alarmed to hear someone use his full name. The only time that ever seems to happen is when there's trouble, or at the very least serious news to be told.

"Hey, this is Jacob, a friend of Jason's, the campground host up at Ahart in French Meadows…"

The man was quickly bringing Nathan up to speed.

Nathan sat up and gulped. He didn't have words.

"Hey, I think we may have your dog," the voice continued.

Nathan had heard those words so many times in the past 20 months, but this time felt different. As images of Murphy flashed through Nathan's mind, the man spoke again.

"Nathan?"

On the other end of the line, Nathan felt dizzy. "Is it a golden retriever?" he stammered, the first question he and Erin had learned to ask so many months before.

"Yes," Jacob replied.

"Is the dog female?" Nathan asked, his guard still up.

"I'm not sure, but Jason thinks it's Murphy. He couldn't get cell reception so he told me to drive into town to give you a call. The dog got away the first time Jason found her, but then last night a few dog treats and a calm voice did the trick. He's got her and wants you to come see for yourself."

Images flooded Nathan's mind as he sat up. Could it really be?

"The crazy thing is, he found her cuddled up on the stuff you left," Jacob continued. "She got away the first time but just to be sure, she's in a borrowed kennel now."

More images crammed Nathan's mind. His thoughts were of Murphy panting and healthy, just as she was when her eyes lit up and her tail wagged happily whenever he'd come through the front door, or even come into the same room.

It was hard to imagine Murphy as anything other than the image he had of her when he last saw her, but his greatest worry at that moment was how badly life in the wild had treated her.

But she's alive! Nathan hoped, remembering just as quickly that there were still hurdles to cross before they could celebrate.

"The people who loaned their kennel have her secured, so she can't get away again," Jacob continued.

How could this be? Nathan thought, in a daze. It's impossible.

"I'll call you back," he stammered to Jacob, feeling too confused to carry on a coherent conversation.

Chapter 48

Silver bars surrounded Murphy, keeping her from freedom. At first she whimpered as she tried to pace in the tight environment, unable to roam freely. The voices that spoke to her were calm and gentle. Then the owners of those voices slipped food to her and gave her fresh water. Murphy calmed down, but as soon as she brushed against the cage it was a reminder that she was enclosed, making her anxiety start all over again

At home, Nathan still wasn't sure what to think. Should he believe the caller? It all seemed like a dream.

"Happy almost Father's Day," Erin called as she walked into the bedroom with a basket of clean laundry on her hip. "Who was that?"

Nathan replied a little too quickly, "Nobody."

He didn't want to let his own hopes get too high, so he certainly couldn't dash his family's.

Or could I? Nathan thought. Could it really be possible?

Nathan knew he could satisfy his curiosity in a couple of hours if he chose to. This was the persistent thought that nagged him, the thought that made him quiet and thoughtful the rest of the morning.

In some ways he really didn't have the luxury to think about it for long. They were packing up to drive to see friends for Father's Day weekend, nearly a two hours' drive southwest; the opposite direction from the mountains.

But as they set out on the road for their getaway weekend, Nathan had time to think about it. The kids, usually boisterous and always up to some sort of childhood game, were quiet on the drive, leaving him alone with his thoughts.

Nathan grew pensive, focusing on the road ahead, not sure what to do or whether he should say anything.

"You okay?" Erin asked, looking over, sunglasses shielding her eyes, but concern in her voice that couldn't be hidden. She'd taken up knitting hats for everyone in the family. It quieted her mind and gave her something to do, especially on those days, or often those nights, when she felt antsy and wanted to put her energy into something. She soon realized that doing something creative is a great way to stay calm, especially when she rode as a passenger.

Erin's voice snapped Nathan out of his reverie, a reminder that he wasn't alone in any of this.

"Hold tight until we get there," he said, looking in the back to see what the kids were up to. Finegan's head drooped over in sleep. Morgan was reading a book and Matthew was looking out the windows, ear buds visible.

"You sure?" Erin said. "What is it?"

Just then the kids perked up as they saw the familiar signs, showing them that they were close to their friends' house. Nathan steered the car into the long driveway. As soon as the kids rolled out of the car, Nathan and Erin stayed behind for an extra minute alone to talk.

Nathan began to pour the whole story out to Erin.

"Someone thinks he may have found Murphy," Nathan explained earnestly, but also calmly. "I think it's a long shot."

His logic told him they'd exhausted the search. It would've been impossible for Murphy to survive for two winters in the wild.

"Seen or found?" Erin asked. She put her knitting down.

"All I know is that they're holding a dog that they think is Murphy," Nathan said.

"Let's get up there!" Erin cried, a sparkle in her eye, ready to take on another quest in what had become a countless string of hunts for their precious pet. After all, she and Nathan were always the ones willing to push on, to keep searching until others told them to stop.

Nathan feared disappointment, not for himself, but in wanting to shield his family from more pain. How many times could he make that drive only to be told that the dog was somebody else's? He kept hearing Erin's voice and the certainty in her eyes, wanting him to go.

I'll do it for her, he thought.

The kids were still busy greeting their family friends. The adult hosts began to make their way toward the car.

Erin and Nathan said the usual "Hello," and "How are you?" gave hugs and handshakes, but within an hour, they shared the news with their friends, all while trying to keep the new development from the kids.

The four of them looked at every angle. When they exhausted all of the possibilities, of whether this mystery dog could really be Murphy, whether they wanted to believe it or not, all signs pointed to yes. They had to make the trip again. They decided, with their friends' blessing, to make the same trip east, across the foothills to the Sierras once again. The Braun family had made the trip so many times during the last 20 months. Would nearly two years without Murphy finally be coming to an end?

Chapter 49

Sunday, June 16, 2014,

Father's Day

The past 20 months had been difficult for all the Brauns, but especially hard on Nathan. It weighed on him that he had been the one to lose Murphy. He was grateful that Erin never blamed him or made him think they were not in it together. But now he was concerned about upsetting his family any further. What if this sighting would lead to more heartbreak? What if it was only false hope that the dog would really be Murphy?

Erin was resolute. When she looked at Nathan her green eyes were fiery and bright. "Why stop now?" she asked.

They both knew what to do next.

They borrowed their friend's kennel and put it in the back before loading the kids in the car. Erin looked at it, dreaming that it would soon carry their dear Murphy back home where she belonged.

"Where are we going?" the kids asked, annoyed that their trip was being cut short and that they couldn't at least stay for breakfast with their friends.

Erin and Nathan weren't ready to share the news. As they thought about what to say, the questions stopped.

Sometime later, when pine trees out the window became plentiful, Matthew asked, "Why aren't we going the usual way home?"

Nathan stopped the car and turned to look at his kids in the back seat.

"Someone is holding a dog that could be Murphy," he told them. Their three faces upturned into smiles. "I need to stop at this bank to get the reward money."

When he shut the door he could hear the whoops and hollers from inside. He couldn't hide his excitement either as he grinned wide.

The family of five continued driving east on Highway 80, the route they'd taken many times before. They'd grown to know every exit, every turn, practically every pothole on the highway. Going to the mountains before Murphy was lost, and since, had been as familiar to them as the blanket and ball cap were to Murphy.

Yet no other time did the drive feel so long. They couldn't wait to see whether the dog was indeed theirs.

Nathan tapped his fingers on the steering wheel and Erin knitted intently. The only sound was the occasional whispering from the kids in the back seat. Silence seemed the only remedy until the first question was asked, then the next, and then another.

"What would Murphy look like if it's her?"

"What did she used to look like?"

"Will she remember us?"

"Will she be scared?"

When the roads began to wind, Erin drove so she wouldn't get carsick. More questions and family discussions followed, always about Murphy.

"What if it's a boy?"

"What if the dog isn't Murphy. Would we take her anyway since this dog is most likely lost too?"

"It's like God is sending us a message that no matter what, we need to do what is right," Erin said. "If the dog isn't Murphy, we will work hard to find its owner, just like we'd hope someone would do for us."

Chapter 50

Before the car had come to a complete stop, Nathan was starting to unbuckle his seat belt. He was more than eager to get out of the car and head for Jason's trailer. Nathan saw his hat and the blanket next to the front door, and then he saw the kennel. Immediately they all ran to the kennel, but once they got close enough to touch it, they saw it was empty.

"Maybe she's gone again," Morgan said as she looked at her parents.

Nathan knocked on Jason's front door, but there was no answer.

"He's probably making his rounds to check on the campsites and took the dog with him," Nathan said.

He jumped back into the car and they drove from campsite to campsite, looking for Jason. Jason had been driving around the campsites, collecting overnight fees and bagging garbage.

They arrived at Lewis Campground and meandered slowly through the campsites until they reached the end. Just as they were about to turn, looping back out the way they had come, Nathan saw Jason's truck. Jason was in the driver's seat and caught their eye.

At once, Erin yelled out the window in his direction. "Is it a girl?"

Without hesitating, Jason yelled back, "Yes!"

They could see the back of his truck and then, the most beautiful sight in the world. They saw the head of a very dirty, very frail golden retriever.

"Look!" Erin called. She was out of the car in an instant.

Nathan hung back, walking in her direction more cautiously. They had told the kids to wait in the car until they were sure, one way or another.

From first impression, Nathan thought the dog in the kennel couldn't be Murphy. When they got closer he was even more sure it wasn't Murphy. This dog was so skinny; her coat and eyes were much lighter than Murphy's. This dog had a yellowish ginger colored coat, not the rich rusty color Murphy had.

Erin reached for the dog, searching her eyes. "My baby," Erin cooed, tears welling in her eyes.

Murphy looked right at her, gave a sigh of relief, relaxation finally possible after so much time having to fend off predators, protect herself, and live in the unknown. That voice, the familiar smells of her family, flooded Murphy's senses. She held up her paw and began to wag her tail the best she could.

She so badly wanted to jump into her family's arms, but she was still tied down for her own safety. Even if she wanted to jump in her mind, her body most likely wouldn't have allowed it. She was weak. The whites of her eyes were pink, discolored from exposure; her fur mangy and dirty. Murphy was completely worn out, yet she had done it. She had survived!

Erin burst into tears. "Murphy!" Erin cried. "Oh my God!" Nearly two years of worry and uncertainty that had built up inside of her exploded in an instant. She took Murphy by the face. Despite the grime and discoloration, there was no doubt it was their Murphy, and Murphy knew she was with her family at last.

Erin continued to kiss and hug Murphy and waved to the kids to come over.

"Murphy!" Morgan called as she approached. Murphy greeted her with another paw lift.

"At first we thought she was a coyote," a camper interrupted. "But then Jason told us to keep a look out for your dog. Once we got a closer look, we could tell it was no coyote."

Jason walked over. He'd been waiting to see this reunion take place and was glad to see there was no doubt. He was surprised by how friendly and energetic the dog was—so different from the dog who had been so skittish before.

"You can tell she knows you," he said. "That's the most she's moved or interacted with anyone."

Murphy was untied by then, licking her family enthusiastically. The smells, the cuddles, the kisses. It was nearly more than she could bear and her tail wagged so hard it looked like it might snap.

"Wow," Jason smiled. Murphy rolled on her side to be touched. "She wouldn't do that for anyone before. Look at that."

Tears streamed down everyone's faces and even the witnesses to the miraculous reunion shed tears. Even Finegan, just a baby when Murphy went missing, said the name that had become part of his limited vocabulary.

"Murph," he cooed, cuddling Murphy close.

Erin was overjoyed. She would later share that the moment ranked the same in happiness as their wedding day, or even the three days her children were born. She was overjoyed.

Nathan still wasn't sure. He wanted it to be Murphy, but this dog looked so different. He stood one foot apart from the action, watching as his family and this dog interacted as though they were inside a bubble and he was standing on the outside, looking in.

There is only one way to find out if this dog is Murphy, Nathan thought.

A man who was camping at the site had a pair of clippers he said Nathan could borrow. Nathan proceeded to shave a section of fur from the dog's right front leg.

"Oh my gosh!" Nathan cried out, dissolving into tears now, too. The mystery was finally solved. There it was—a long scar Murphy had gotten when she was a puppy, right where Nathan hoped it would be, as much proof this dog was Murphy as anything. The scar was the most beautiful sight Nathan could imagine.

Nathan and Erin looked at each other and smiled, both thinking, *How on earth?*

"Thank you," Nathan said to Jason. He reached in his pocket to offer Jason the reward, the money that had practically burned a hole in his wallet, he had wanted so badly to be able to give it away.

"Nah," Jason waved it off. "You're going to need it for vet bills."

Chapter 51

Once the family piled back into the car to make their last trip home, the one they'd dreamed about, the three kids kept talking to Murphy, stroking her, telling her how much they had missed her. Murphy's eyes grew heavy. She fell asleep to the sounds of their voices.

Erin kept looking back to make sure that Murphy was really there. It wasn't a prank. They actually had her with them, finally! She picked up her phone to text their family and friends. *Do you believe in miracles?*

THE BRAUN FAMILY – JUNE, 2014

Afterword

Murphy's physical transformation from living in the wild was startling. The Brauns' veterinarian said Murphy's lighter fur and darkened pigment in the whites of her eyes were similar to what happens when people are either malnourished, get too much sun exposure, or both. Yet within days of being home Murphy's coat began growing darker and her eyes grew more clear.

The Brauns spent the first few days reconnecting with Murphy. When they first got home they took Murphy into the house in a kennel. They thought she would feel safer in it. They were scared she might run off again. After about fifteen minutes of little movement, they opened the door to see what would happen. Nathan's mother, Carmen, sat on the edge of the lawn. Murphy walked out of the kennel and walked delicately over to Grandma Braun. She gave Grandma a few sniffs and then began to kiss her face all over.

The local and national news media, even the British Broadcasting Corporation (BBC), covered the miraculous story of the dog who came home after going missing for nearly two years in the wild.

Tired and frail, many of Murphy's old mannerisms resurfaced, with only a few changes. She didn't want to go near the pool, let alone jump into it, and she didn't want to be left alone or let outside unless someone went with her. Who could blame her?

At first she was skittish about sleeping between Erin and Nathan again, a habit she'd grown to love before. Yet soon she was back where she belonged and for the first time in nearly two years all three of them slept well.

The children continued to look for proof that the found dog was indeed Murphy. "The hard spot on her head's the same," Matthew said. "That's how I know it's her."

"She has the same spots on her nose," 10-year-old Morgan said.

Little three-year-old Finegan, too young to understand the ordeal Murphy had endured, threw a ball to play catch while Murphy just stared at it.

"She was never a good fetcher," Nathan said, smiling. "It's kind of like someone returning from the dead," he continued, still in awe days after the reunion.

The first 72 hours of her homecoming, the Brauns separated Murphy from their younger golden retriever, Lambeau, who'd been so depressed after Murphy went missing. "We were wondering if Murphy would be aggressive at all after living in the wild for so long," Nathan explained.

They also wanted to get Murphy checked for heartworm and parasites, and they had an identifying microchip placed inside her so they could never lose her again. When Murphy's check-up came back clean except for being very skinny, they reunited her with Lambeau.

"They started wagging tails and sniffing each other," Erin remembered. "It was like Lambeau was saying, 'I know you and I also know you're not feeling well.'"

Murphy never showed any aggression toward Lambeau or the children.

Still, the miracle of how Murphy survived remains a mystery and the motivation to write this book. Was it the two mild winters that enabled her to search the campgrounds for food? Why did such a water lover come home afraid of it? What happened to Murphy's collar? The Brauns theorize that humans must have come in contact with Murphy, possibly even caring for her at some point, thus the motivation to create the Paj and Drake characters.

One thing is certain. "Her camping days are over," Nathan said.

Instead, Murphy enjoys staying home with her

family and talking walks around the neighborhood.

What is the lesson Erin and Nathan will continue to teach their children about the family's harrowing experience and miraculous reunion? "Persistence and hope can pay off," they said. "We never gave up. It reinforced our belief in God, to have faith and to never give up hope. We are forever grateful for Murphy's life."

Acknowledgments — Written by Erin and Nathan Braun

We have so many individual people to thank—the list is endless. Words cannot describe how grateful we are. Homeward Bound Golden Retriever Rescue was instrumental in their efforts to help, as well as the campground host.

It's because of every person's efforts that the hiker could first track us down. It wasn't just one person. It was all the people who helped for even an hour.

You all know who you are. Thank you from the bottom of our hearts. We are forever grateful.

Discussion Questions

1. Many people today consider their pets to be part of their family. Paj's parents don't agree with this view. They see dogs as possessions, or workers for their family. Which opinion do you agree with?

2. Do you think a domestic dog could survive in the wilderness for almost two years? Why, or why not?

3. Although dogs and coyotes are related, coyotes are wild animals and dogs are not. Do you think a coyote pack would accept a dog into their group?

4. Many dogs are trained as "therapy dogs" and help soldiers such as Drake. Do you think dogs can provide emotional support to people?

5. Do you think you would recognize your dog if it had been missing as long as Murphy had been, and if it had gone through as many physical changes as Murphy had?

6. Wolverines haven't been sighted in the Sierra Nevada since the 1920s, but one has been sighted in recent years. What other animals in the book seemed mysterious to you or would you like to know more about?

7. What would you do if one of your family members got lost or hurt while you were in charge?

8. How would you survive in the wild if you were left with nothing but the clothes on your back?

9. Why do you think it was important for the Brauns to not give up hope? Has there been a time in your life when you were challenged like this?

10. Besides physical changes, how did Murphy change from the beginning of the book to the end?

ABOUT THE AUTHOR

Julie Samrick is a journalist and author living in El Dorado County, California. She holds a degree in English from UC Berkeley.

You can connect with Julie at her website and on social media. Be sure to subscribe to her newsletter, so you'll be the first to hear about her new books.

www.JulieSamrick.com